The Wrong Roommate

The Wrong Roommate

Tea City Rollers

Alby Blake

Content Expectations

- Foul language, dirty talk, and spicy situations
- Fear of thunderstorms
- Pretending spicy situations never happened

Chapter One

My shoulder hurts. I roll it, knowing it's going to have a nasty bruise on it tomorrow. If it's still sore in a week, I'll swing by the team's medic and have them take a look, but in the meantime, I still have my full range of motion so I'm not worried. Besides, the only heavy lifting I'll be doing tonight is raising my drink to my lips.

This house party is packed. I snag a craft beer from the garage fridge. It's not the wine I prefer, but this isn't a wine type of party. Then I make my way through the house, scanning the crowd for Rafe.

"Sera!"

I turn and spot Daphne's strawberry blond hair in the corner, where she's nursing a beer of her own. I push through the crowd until I reach her and squeeze onto the window bench next to her.

"Why do you come to these huge parties if you always spend the entire time hiding in a corner?" I ask her as I settle in. Daphne isn't on the team, but we've been best friends for so long that she's as much a part of the group as I am. I've tried to get her to join, but she's not into the part where we end up battered and bruised after every bout. Not that I blame her. Daphne has her own thing going as a competitive jigsaw puzzler, which I didn't know was a thing until I met her, but she's incredible at it. And let's be honest, puzzling is much kinder to one's body than roller derby, and as dedicated as she is to it, she wouldn't have time to do both.

There's a group of my teammates and friends already watching a replay of today's bout in the living room and even though I can hear their commentary, it's mostly drowned out by the party noise. Which is fine by me. I'm not ready to see a video of my hit yet. My shoulder is all the reminder I need for tonight.

Daphne shrugs. "Everyone else seems to have a good time, and I like the people-watching."

"You should have fun too," I tell her. "Maybe find Rowan and get your flirt on."

Daphne ignores my attempt at matchmaking. "How's your shoulder?"

"Nothing a beer or two won't fix." I give her the side-eye, wondering how she knows about my injury. I know for a fact that she wasn't at our match this afternoon since she had told me yesterday she couldn't get the time off from the bookstore.

As though she can read my mind, Daphne says, "This is the second play-through of the bout footage." She nods toward the living room. "That hit looked brutal."

I nod and change the subject. "How long has Rowan been missing from his own party?" If Daphne has already been here long enough to see the entire bout through once, she must have gotten here early. Probably to try to get up the guts to talk to our team manager.

She's been in love with our team manager, Rowan, for two years now, but mostly pines from afar despite my efforts to encourage her to actually talk to him. Not only do I want to see my friend get what she wants, because she deserves to be happy, but I also know that if she can just get past her shyness and actually talk to the man, he'll become just as smitten with her as she is with him, which would be good for everyone, especially the female population of the greater Portland area. He's a great guy, but he's a shameless flirt and his body count is higher than any other person I've ever met.

His only rule is no players, which is great news for Daphne—if she would just come out of her shell enough for him to notice her.

We sit in a comfortable best-friends silence for a while, watching the crowd mingle.

"Rafe is here," Daphne suddenly says, taking a casual sip of her beer.

I sit up straighter and roll my shoulders back, which draws my attention back to my bruise for a moment as I try to act casual. My friend's snort lets me know I'm failing.

"He got here maybe half an hour before you," she continues. "Came alone."

All I can do is nod and smooth my hair back, glad I washed it before coming over instead of just air-drying the sweat and then yanking it into a messy topknot. Freshly washed, the matcha green highlights really pop, which is a real confidence booster. My stomach is full of butterflies, which is silly because I see Rafe all the time. We've known each other for five years, he and Rowan are good friends, and he works at Drizzle & Drip, my favorite café. Yet every time I see him, I feel like a teenager catching a glimpse of her crush.

"He's in the kitchen. Maybe you should go say hi." Daphne's demeanor hasn't changed, so if I didn't know her as well as I do, I'd think she was just making a suggestion. But she's definitely issuing a challenge.

"Maybe I will." I tug at the neckline of my shirt to make

sure it offers up a good view of my cleavage without going overboard.

"I don't see you moving," Daphne taunts me.

"Fuck you," I whisper, but there's no heat in it. I know exactly why she's pushing me—the same reason I push her to talk to Rowan—and I know she's right. I just can't make my stupid body stand up and walk to the kitchen, where I'll find Rafe's sexy, lumberjack-looking self surrounded by a group of women vying for his attention.

"No thanks," Daphne says with a smile. "You're not my type. So why are you still here?"

Sticking out my tongue at her like a mature adult, I square my shoulders and move off toward the kitchen. If I just listen for the sound of incessant giggling, it's sure to lead me directly to Rafe. There's something magnetic about him. Women flock to him no matter where he is. It probably has something to do with his broad shoulders and the way the tendons in his arms flex when he moves. Not to mention his smile. His gorgeous, calming, draws-you-in-and-makes-you-wet smile.

Sure enough, I find him with four women, all trying their best to impress him. Not that I can blame them. He looks fantastic in a cream button-up with the sleeves rolled up. It's just thin enough to see the faint lines of his tattoos underneath. *Swoon.*

Pausing by the drinks table, I pretend to consider the liquor options while planning my next move. If I've learned anything from derby, it's to examine the herd for gaps to block out the jammers and ensure they don't get the point. Or in this case, the guy.

"Sera!" a deep male voice calls out.

I look up sharply, confused. Deep male voices don't usually call my name from across the room. I'm not unpopular, but I'm kind of a wallflower. Definitely not the girl whose attention the guys try to get.

"Sera!" Rafe raises his arm to wave at me over the heads of his adoring crowd. "Excuse me, ladies."

He flashes them one of his patented dimpled smiles and begins to make his way over to me. His fan club leaves him very little room to get past them, forcing him to brush up against them. I suppose I should be charitable and assume they give him a normal amount of space and he's just such a big dude it looks like they're trying to keep him there, but the way one of them snakes a hand across his abdomen as he squeezes by her indicates my initial assessment was probably on the money.

All I can do is stand there and try to look like a hot guy coming over to me of his own volition is a normal occurrence for me. I glance over at Daphne to see that she's just as surprised as I am by this turn of events. I try to smooth my features into an expression that says *Nice to see you* rather than *Holy shit, you're talking to me.*

"Hey, I'm so glad you're here." Rafe flashes me not only one, but both dimples, and I decide to give the abs-touching woman a pass after all. "Question for you: you've just moved into your new house, right?"

I mentally tick off the items that have left me flabbergasted in the past thirty seconds: Rafe noticed me on his own, Rafe left his bevy of admirers to talk to me, Rafe is glad I'm here, and now Rafe is remembering details from my personal life? I suppose I have been talking about it a lot recently—I'm pretty proud of the fact that I've been able to buy a house all by myself at twenty-seven, and I've been putting a lot of work into decorating and making it mine so it really feels like home—but I'm surprised he's been paying that much attention.

"Yeah, about a month and a half ago."

"Nice! How many bedrooms did you say it was again?"

That's...a bit of a specific question. I'm about to point that out when Rafe smiles again, and I decide he can be as specific as he wants as long as he keeps flashing those dimples. "Three, but the one on the main floor is super small so I just turned it into a little office."

He nods, more to himself than to me. "Cool. Are you using the second one as, like, a guest room or anything?"

Even the dimples aren't enough to distract me from the oddness of this line of questioning, but I don't know how to point out that he's being weird. "Not yet. I'd love to set it up as a guest room someday, but I figured I'd finish the other rooms where I actually live first." I force myself to stop there. I don't want to go down the homeowner rabbit hole. I'd definitely bore Rafe then.

"So, you do have an extra bedroom?" He rubs the back of his neck, looking a little uncomfortable. It's weird, he's usually so confident, and I'm trying to think of a way to get him to get to the point when he asks, "Any chance you'd be open to a roommate?"

I blink, not sure I heard him correctly. A roommate? Rafe, my crush of the past year, with the sexy forearm tendons and double dimples, is asking if he can be my roommate?

He's still talking. "I mean, if you don't want to share your space, I get it. You just moved in, you're still making the place your own, but if you'd be open to it, I'm kind of in a bind with—"

Rafe wants to move in with me. Rafe! Wants to move in! With me! "I would be open to having a roommate," I say, cutting him off. I'd be an idiot not to say yes to this. "Of course. No point in letting the room sit empty."

"Are you sure? It sounds like you had a plan for it, I'd hate for this to derail that."

I wave a dismissive hand. "That's, like, a way-down-the-road plan. I was going to do the basement next anyway, and I have a pull-out couch so there's a spot for guests to sleep." This isn't entirely true, as the basement will likely be a more expensive undertaking than a guest room would be so it would probably have come later, but whatever. I don't really have overnight guests often anyway.

Rafe's shoulders relax and his nervousness is replaced with his usual good humor. "Really? Oh, that's awesome. You're a lifesaver. Thanks so much, Sera, really." Rafe's giant arms envelop me. The hug all but lifts me off the floor, he's so much bigger than I am.

"Of course," I repeat as he releases me, dizzy with the faint scent of wood that clings to his skin and the feel of his arms around me. "So, what kind of timeframe are you thinking as far as a move-in date?"

"Sooner the better, honestly. Any chance tomorrow would work?" I must look like that shocked-Pikachu meme because his expression turns sheepish. "That's probably way too soon, isn't it? Sorry. It doesn't have to be tomorrow, I just got excited. A guy can only crash on his friend's couch for so long, you know? Especially when it's just a normal couch, not a pull-out."

"Oh, ah." That is so much sooner than I thought. I really should sit down and think this through before committing. What if we don't get along? What if he's a complete slob? I don't need the house to be spotless all the time, but I will be seriously grossed out if I constantly find smelly guy socks on the sofa or puddles of milk on the counter. And if he's been sleeping on a friend's couch, does he have furniture in storage or something? I don't have spare furniture. I don't even have an air mattress. And what about rent? And utilities? How are we going to figure all of that out?

But it's Rafe. He's cute and smells good and is generally just nice. He's got a steady job, and he always looks put-together, no stains on his clothes or anything to make me think he's the type to spill something and not clean it up. I've had a crush on him practically since I moved here. If he wants to move in tomorrow, he must really be in a tight spot. If it were Daphne, I'd say yes without a second thought. Why should it be any different with Rafe? He's my friend too. And it does sound like he needs a new living situation fast.

Rafe's fan club is closing in on us, hovering at the edge of our conversation. I can feel them wanting to jump in and offer to let him move in with them. I can't let that happen. If Rafe moves in with me, maybe the crush I've been harboring will finally turn into something more. There are tons of romance novels and movies where that's the whole plot, right? Two people being forced to live together or stay in the same hotel or sit next to each other at work, and they end up falling in love after spending all that time in each other's company?

I need to cinch this win fast, before the fan club has a chance to pounce.

"Sure, why not? Tomorrow sounds great." If I take the time to consider all the potential implications, I'll waffle until one of Rafe's groupies swoops in and I miss my chance. If nothing else, now that I'll have Rafe contributing to the household expenses, I can put the money I'm saving toward getting the basement finished and ready to double as a guest room.

I should probably go home immediately and clean everything so that when he arrives tomorrow, I can nonchalantly pretend that my house always looks fantastic. Maybe if it looks perfect when he first gets there it'll dissuade him from leaving dirty laundry in the common areas, if he's inclined that way.

"Awesome! You're the best. Seriously, you have no idea what a relief this is." Rafe flashes me those dimples again, and the girls who were fawning over him earlier all give me the stink-eye. "See you tomorrow, probably late afternoon, then."

"See you then," I say cheerily before turning back to where Daphne is waiting for me. When I glance back at Rafe, the party crowd has already swallowed him up, creating a solid wall of people several feet deep between us.

"You will never believe what just happened," I whisper-squeal to Daphne when I get back to our corner. I do a quick little happy dance before reclaiming my spot on the bench.

"Tell me!" Daphne claps excitedly. "What did he want? He looked intense when he was talking to you."

"He asked to move in with me!" I still can't believe it. I've been trying to get Rafe to notice me for ages, and this is more than I could have ever hoped for.

"He asked to *move in* with you?" I'd expected Daphne to be thrilled, but she looks confused and a little skeptical.

I take a sip of my now-warm drink. Ew. No more of that, I decide. "Well, he asked if I'd be open to a roommate, since I have an extra bedroom in my house. I guess he's been sleeping on a friend's couch for a bit."

"How did that happen?"

I shrug, immediately regretting it as my shoulder twinges with the movement. "No clue. Does it matter? If it hadn't happened, he wouldn't be moving in with me tomorrow."

"*Tomorrow?* Isn't that a little fast? What if he's sleeping on a couch because he's a terrible roommate who never pays rent and he got kicked out of his last place?"

Annoyed that my friend won't just be happy for me, I make a face at her. "Can you really see Rafe being the type to not pay his rent?"

"I don't know. Maybe not. I'm just saying, it's kind of weird that he wants to move in immediately."

I gesture at the other room, where we can see Rafe towering over the crowd. "The man is like six-five, and he's been sleeping on a sofa. I'd be desperate to find a new place too if I were him."

She takes a drink as she considers this. "Okay, that's fair."

I grab her hand and squeeze it. "Just be happy for me, Daph," I wheedle. "This is the stuff romcoms are made of. He's going to move in and fall madly in love with me and we're going to get married and live happily ever after."

"You know this means you're going to have to look cute all the time," she warns me.

I let go of her hand. "Fuck. You're right. I didn't even think about that." Now I have to clean the whole house *and* do laundry so I can ensure I have cute outfits for the next few days. "I should go. I have a lot to get done in the next eighteen hours."

I head into the kitchen to dump my drink and throw the bottle in the recycling bin—maybe other people would just leave it on a table somewhere for Rowan to clean up later, but that feels wrong to me. I make my way back through the house to the front door, and when I pull it open, Rafe looks over at me and waves. "See you tomorrow, Sera."

I wave back. "Yeah, see you." I close the door behind me, dampening the party noise, and I can't help the grin that spreads across my face as I whisper into the night, *"Roomie."*

Chapter Two

My house officially looks fantastic. Well, except for my bedroom. That looks like a tornado just went through, but I closed the door so Rafe will never know. I'll clean it later. But at least the rest of the house is spotless and will hopefully impresses him. I don't want him to change his mind about moving in.

I can barely contain my nervous excitement, checking out the front windows every five minutes. When I see his beat-up red truck pull up in front of my house, I squeal and do a full-on happy dance. This might be the last time for a while that no one is here to see me dweeb out like this, I have to take advantage.

When I hear the truck door close, I take a few deep, calming breaths the way I would before a bout, then open the door with poise and a smile.

A smile which disappears when a second car, a shiny silver Prius with a cat hanging from the rearview mirror, pulls into my driveway. My stomach drops into my sneakers and my blood begins to boil. I know exactly who that car belongs to, and he's not welcome here. What is he even doing back in Portland, anyway? I thought I'd finally gotten rid of him when he moved to California last year.

As Jakub Lattner steps out of his car, my fingers tighten on the doorknob and I have a sudden burning desire to race down the walkway and shove him to the ground—two handed, the way I would never be allowed to in roller derby.

Instead, I tell myself that maybe he's just visiting and came along to help Rafe move in. The bedroom furniture I can see in the back of Rafe's truck looks really solid and heavy, so I suppose it would be a good idea to have another set of hands to help move it. Jakub can do some heavy lifting and then get out of my house immediately. I'm not spending my first night with Rafe entertaining Jakub fucking Lattner.

No, tonight it's just going to be me and Rafe.

Alone.

"Hey there." Rafe lumbers up the driveway and gathers me up in a hug.

"Hi." I'm not normally a hugger, but I close my eyes and lean into it. He's so big his arms could probably wrap around me twice, and his flannel button-up smells like the forests on a cool day, all pine and sun and clear running water.

"Thanks for agreeing to this, and so quick too," he says as he releases me. As he moves away, I can see Jakub, his dark hair in disarray as he casually leans back against his car, watching the exchange.

"No worries. I'm glad to help." Maybe one day, when we're an old married couple. I'll tell him that I only let him move in because I was hoping he'd fall madly in love with me and we'd live happily ever after. But for now, I'm going to keep letting him think I'm just being selfless.

Rafe turns to Jakub. "All right, let's start with the bigger furniture. We can figure out where they go and then move the smaller things in behind them." He heads back to his truck, clearly expecting Jakub to follow his lead like most people do.

But Jakub doesn't move. "Sounds like a plan," he calls, still watching me. One side of his mouth quirks up, and I just know he's going to do everything in his power to irritate me while he's here. He always does.

Jakub and I have been rivals since we were in the same graphic design program back in college, always vying for the same internships and one-upping each other in grades and professor feedback. We both ended up in Portland after graduation despite neither of us being from here, because of course we did, and it was college all over again. He swept in and landed the job at the Bachman Agency that I was sure I was a shoo-in for, forcing me to take a much lower-paying one at Amplifi.

A year later, Amplifi went under and I found myself unemployed for almost two months before an amazing position opened at KLR Digital. It was truly my dream job, even better than the one at Bachman that I'd lost to him. When I got an interview, I cried actual tears of happiness. When I got a second interview, Daphne and I went out for celebratory cupcakes at the expensive bakery we loved but could rarely justify going to. When I got a third interview, this time with the president of the company, and the HR coordinator I'd been working with told me it was pretty much just a formality, I popped a half-sized bottle of bubbly and drank it straight from the bottle while sitting in a bubble bath and singing along to "Don't Stop Me Now".

When the HR coordinator called me to tell me that the president had decided to go with someone else, I was shocked. Although I shouldn't have been. Of course Jakub jumped ship from Bachman to snap up the job that I not only wanted more than I'd ever wanted a job before, but that I desperately needed.

And of course, by then I was overqualified for the entry-level position he'd just vacated at Bachman, so I couldn't even have a second go at that. It was like Jakub and the universe had sat down for lunch with the president of KLR and said, "How can we best destroy Sera's life this week?"

Thank fuck for Daphne. She knew I'd been saving to buy a house of my own since I moved to Portland, so she suggested that I move in with her for a while instead of renewing my apartment lease so I wouldn't burn through all my savings. Everyone should have a Daphne in their lives.

I ended up crashing on her couch for months until I finally, *finally* got hired at AdX. It was a smaller and less well-known ad agency, but it was up-and-coming and my new boss, Jocelyn, was amazing. She was young and full of exciting ideas, and encouraged all of us to pitch our own ideas and really make the team feel like a collaborative unit. For a while, I even thought that maybe I could forgive Jakub for the KLR thing, because I'd ended up with something so much better than I could have ever dreamed. I looked forward to going to work each day, Daphne and I decided to get an apartment together so I could have an actual room again, and I was making good money that allowed me to start saving up to buy my house now that I was paying half as much in rent as I'd been when I lived alone.

And last year, Jakub moved away with his girlfriend. Our professional rivalry may have finally fizzled out, but I was still glad to never have to see him again. No more Jakub showing up at derby parties because Rafe invited him to hang out with us. No more running into him at Drizzle & Drip because again, he was friends with Rafe. No more hearing his name come up at work when we lost a bid to KLR, or seeing designs around town that I knew were his because after four years in the same program at school, I recognized when a client had let him put some of his hallmarks into a design.

Finally, I was free of Jakub Lattner, I loved my job, and life couldn't have been better.

For three months.

Then Jocelyn's sommelier wife got a dream opportunity in Napa that she couldn't turn down. Which meant my amazing boss who made my job something to look forward to every day was leaving.

Unfortunately, AdX didn't find Jocelyn 2.0 to take her place; they found Bartholomew. Bartholomew, who must have majored in Micromanagement and minored in Not Listening to His Employees, with a focus on Growing the Department Too Fast and Burning Us All Out. Bartholomew, who made AdX suddenly no better to work for than any other agency. Bartholomew, who made me wish I'd studied something else in school. I should have changed majors the day I walked into my first design class to find Jakub already sucking up to the professor.

And now, after all that, he has the nerve to come back to Portland and show up at my house? If it weren't for the fact that we need the extra hands to move Rafe's heavy furniture, I'd tell him to get off my property and back out of my life for good.

I flip him the bird and move to follow Rafe.

"Charming," says Jakub dryly as he falls in behind me.

I ignore him. Insulting his friend in front of him is probably not the way to Rafe's heart.

But really, Rafe needs better friends.

"Let's carry up this dresser first, then we can get to the bed frame," says Rafe, climbing up into the truck bed. "Jakub, grab the other side to help lower it down, then we'll carry it in together. Sera, why don't you carry in a drawer, two if you can manage, and go in ahead of us to prop open doors."

He's so sexy when he's in charge. Confident and tall, and strong. *So* strong.

"Gotcha." I accept two drawers from him, one in each hand. They're a lot heavier than I thought they would be. But he builds bespoke wooden furniture, so I guess it's unsurprising for his own furniture to be solid and well-made.

"You sure you got that?" asks Rafe, his voice full of concern as he watches me balance the drawers.

"I'm good. I'm a derby girl, remember?" I say with a wink, glad I've been weightlifting lately to keep strong for derby. Otherwise, I'd probably be embarrassing myself right now.

Jakub just stares at me as I walk past him and head back up to the front porch, for which I'm thankful. If he had made a nasty comment, I'm not sure I would have been able to hold myself back from throttling him, even with Rafe standing right there.

But it's taking them long enough to gently lift the dresser down from the truck bed that I have time to take the drawers upstairs individually. They'll never know.

When I come downstairs from bringing up the second one, the guys are at the front door with the heavy piece of furniture balanced between them. I move aside, holding the door open.

"It's the first door on the right once you're upstairs." Which should be self-explanatory—it's the only open door. I double-checked that I'd closed mine before I came downstairs, not wanting to showcase the disaster zone of a mess inside.

I'm actually a little surprised Rafe hadn't even wanted to come upstairs and see the room first. He must be desperate to get out of whatever living situation he's leaving.

"Thanks," says Rafe, walking backwards up the stairs with his end of the dresser.

When Jakub passes, he gives me the briefest of weird looks and a quick glance around like he's looking for a booby trap. I roll my eyes and head back out to the truck to grab another pair of drawers. I might as well be useful and take the smaller things while they carry all the really heavy furniture.

The next time all three of us are in the entryway again, they've just finished getting the last piece of furniture upstairs. Rafe takes a moment to rest, setting his hands on his waist and looking around the corner into the main area of the house.

I'm even more aware of each of my design choices as Rafe's woodworker's eye takes in the space. The deep emerald of the walls. The gold accent pieces. The modern Victorian loveseat and accent chair, both in strong jewel tones.

"This place looks great, Sera," he says. "I can see your personality come through with the way you've got it set up and decorated."

"Thanks!" As a furniture designer, Rafe has a real eye for that sort of thing, so coming from him this means a lot. "Now that I'm not the only one living here, though, I'm willing to compromise and make the house ours." I want him to know that he can make himself at home here—it's not just my house anymore.

"You're willing to compromise, huh?" asks Jakub, rubbing a hand over his jaw. I swear it looks like he's quietly laughing at me behind his hand.

Why is he still here, anyway? We've gotten everything out of Rafe's truck. He should just leave already.

"See, this right here is why you're so amazing, Sera," says Rafe. "Immediate move-in, compromising on design— we really appreciate how flexible you're being about all of this."

I can feel myself practically preening under Rafe's praise. I only wish Jakub weren't here watching us. He's ruining the vibe.

It takes a second for me to register that Rafe just said *we*, not *I*, and the back of my neck begins to prickle with uncertainty. But he's already moved on and is digging his keys out of his pocket.

"All right, well, looks like you two have everything under control. I'm going to take off. Glad to have you home, buddy, and off my sofa," says Rafe, clasping Jakub's hand with his and pulling him into a bro-hug with his other arm. "Thanks again for letting Jakub move in, Sera. You're the best."

Wait.

What?

Did he just say...

What the fuck?

I stand there, frozen, Rafe's words tumbling around in my head as he wraps me in a slightly sweaty hug and then walks out the door, leaving me alone with the last person I ever want to be alone with.

Jakub looks over at me as Rafe disappears down the driveway and laughs—a real laugh, not the scoffs and snorts he's been tossing over his shoulder at me all afternoon.

"Yeah, thanks for letting me move in, roomie." He claps me on the shoulder and starts toward his car. "Want to help me move in the last few things?"

A strangled sound escapes me and I feel like my legs are about to give out. "I—what?"

"I have a few things left in my backseat that need to be

unloaded." Jakub gestures to his car, where I can see a few boxes are through the window. "Come help me."

"No. What? No. You're not supposed to be here." My head is swimming. Surely I've missed something. Rafe is going to drive back around the corner any minute and yell "Gotcha!" Right? This can't be real.

"Okay, I'll take the bait," says Jakub, opening his car door to grab a box. "Where am I supposed to be?"

"Anywhere but here!" It comes out much louder than I intend, and I blanch, looking around to see if any of the neighbors are outside. I'm still new to the neighborhood and haven't even met them all yet. I want them to like me, not view me as a source of gossip.

"Sera, you've been helping me move in all afternoon," says Jakub as he shoulders past me to bring the box inside. "Why are you acting like this is a huge surprise?"

"I thought Rafe was moving in and you were just helping him," I splutter, following him into the house. "Why would I want you to move in? I don't like you. And you don't like me."

Ahead of me, Jakub snorts. "I had wondered why you were okay with letting me move in, and so quickly too," he says. "I thought maybe you'd decided to finally let go of that immature rivalry from school since I moved away." He deposits the box in the living room—this had better not be him testing me about being willing to compromise on decor —and brushes past me toward the door.

Is he seriously calling me childish? Hello! I own my own home, and he's the one who had to get a friend to find him a place to live because said friend didn't want to live with him anymore. "I'm very mature, thank you very much."

"I can totally tell by the way you're handling this

situation right now." Jakub rolls his eyes again as he jogs back down the porch steps to his car.

Mature or not, I'm not helping him move the rest of his stuff inside. If I'd known it was his stuff before, I wouldn't have helped in the first place. I would have told Rafe that no, I'm not taking on any roommates at the moment. Especially not ones named Jakub Lattner.

Instead, I fold my arms and watch resentfully as Jakub carries another box inside and sets it on the floor in the living room next to the first one.

He returns to his car a final time as I mentally play back over the conversation Rafe and I had at the party. Sure, my brain was a bit addled by the surprise of Rafe seeking me out and *asking to move in* with me, but I absolutely would have noticed if Jakub's name was mentioned. Rafe definitely made it sound like *he* needed a new living situation.

"You can't live here." I resist the urge to stomp my foot to emphasize my words.

Jakub sets the last box down on top of the pile in the living room, then rests an elbow on top of the tower he's made. "So you want me to call Rafe and make him come back to load all my furniture back up? I should move back to Rafe's couch and tell all of your friends that you agreed to let me move in, but now you're backing out after"—Jakub checks his watch theatrically—"less than twenty minutes of us being here alone together?"

I grind my teeth. Daphne wouldn't judge me for hitting "return to sender" on this whole fiasco, because she knows our whole history and how badly he screwed me over with the KLR thing, but what about the rest of my teammates? What about Rafe? I don't want him to think I'm someone who goes back on my word. It wasn't exactly a secret before he left Portland that Jakub and I don't get along, but I don't think most people realized how much I hate him.

"Don't you have any other friends you can mooch off of?" I ask, my hands curling into fists. "Or better yet, you could go back to wherever you were for the past year and a half."

I nearly threw a party when I found out Jakub moved out to California. Him showing up at my house today was the first that I'd even learned of him being back up north, let alone back in town.

Figures, since I've started casually looking for a new job. Of course he'd move back just in time pick up where he left off in ruining my career.

"No one else has an extra room. You're the only one who was living all by your lonesome, everybody else has a partner or friend to keep them company."

"You know what, you're an asshole." I turn on my heel and head for the stairs. "Stay away from me."

"Don't be pissed just because you didn't ask any questions before allowing someone to move in with you," he calls after me. "Be less desperate!"

"I'm desperate?" I lean down over the railing so he can see me point my finger harshly at him. "I'm not the one who had to find a place to live with zero notice because my friend got sick of me taking up space on his couch. I own my house!"

"Lucky you! That house now comes with a roommate!"

I stomp into my bedroom and slam the door shut behind me. Maybe if I make enough noise, he'll be so annoyed he'll move back out. My home is supposed to be a place where I can relax and not have to worry about the stressors of the world, and now the biggest one has just moved in with me.

Chapter Three

I wake up the next morning hoping it was all a bad dream. That yesterday is actually today, and Rafe is mere hours away from pulling up in his truck and unloading his *own* furniture.

But when I open my bedroom door, my hopes crash to the ground. The door to the spare bedroom is closed when I usually keep it open, which can only mean that someone else has closed it. And the only someone that could be is the someone who now, apparently, lives there.

Pausing outside of the door, I lean in and listen for sounds of life on the other side, but I don't hear anything. Either Jakub is still asleep, or he's gone already. I don't even know if he's working right now. I'm kicking myself for not asking more questions when Rafe approached me with this whole idea. Or any questions. I spent last night staring at the ceiling, replaying the whole conversation with him and examining it from every angle. While I can't believe that he didn't tell me outright that he wasn't asking about a room for himself, I can't deny that I'm partly to blame for all of this. I immediately leaped to fantasies about cozy movie nights and cooking dinner together, and didn't even think to double-check that it was, in fact, Rafe who would be starring in these scenarios.

I'm an idiot.

I speed through my morning routine, just in case Jakub is still here. I dress even more professionally than I normally would, so if I have to see him I give the impression that I'm very important at work, and pour my coffee into a thermos with a "Fonts I Have versus Fonts I Use" sticker on it, instead of enjoying it at the kitchen table like I usually do.

I'm a strong, independent woman. I own my house, I'm good at my job, and I hold the cards in this stupid scenario. I just have to figure out how to play them.

I'm going to win this. Fuck Jakub Lattner.

As soon as I step out my front door and onto the porch though, that entire sentiment changes. Fuck *me*.

I throw my bag in the front passenger seat and settle my thermos in the center console before heading back inside and up the stairs. I was really hoping to avoid having to see him, but I have no other choice.

Raising my fist, I knock on Jakub's bedroom door. I want to bang on it, but I restrain myself.

When he doesn't immediately answer, I knock again. Harder this time. If I have to do it again, I'll let myself bang on it.

I'm raising my hand to pound on the door, thinking maybe I'll even allow myself to yell through it, when there's shuffling behind the door and Jakub cracks it open, shoving half his body into the opening so all I can see is one bare leg, one side of his boxers, and his stubbled jaw line. With his eyes hooded from sleep and his hair sticking up, he actually looks like a normal human instead of the smug asshole he usually is. It throws me off for a moment and I stand there blinking at him, forgetting why I'm here.

"Unless you're bringing me breakfast in bed, go away," he grumbles, his voice hoarse, and I snap back to myself.

Bedhead or not, he's still Jakub.

"Your car is in the way and I need to go to work." He's still blocking me from being able to see past him, and I briefly wonder if he's got a woman in there. I'm not sure if I'm more pissed off that he'd bring someone back to my house the first night or grossed out at the idea of someone actually being willing to sleep with him.

"Okay." Jakub looks back into his bedroom, not moving.

"Now! I can't be late for work." I turn and start down the stairs, conscious of Jakub going back into his room before following behind me.

We're going to have to figure out how to avoid this scenario in the future. Not that this living situation is going to last any longer than it absolutely has to, but he can't block me in in my own driveway every day until I manage to get him out of my house.

Sliding into my driver's seat, I glance at my rearview mirror and what I see makes my blood boil. Jakub is out here in front of my house, moving his car in nothing but a pair of boxers. He couldn't at least throw on a pair of pants or a T-shirt?

What are my neighbors going to say? I'll have to come up with a way to leak that he's just a temporary tenant and not my boyfriend or anything. And I'll have to make sure he understands how inappropriate it is to walk around outside my house in his underwear.

Even if he does look halfway decent without a shirt. He's no Rafe, but even as much as I hate him, I can't deny that he's pretty fit.

Ew. I can't believe I even had that thought. Jakub Lattner is not fit, or halfway decent-looking, or anything but an asshole.

As soon as Jakub moves his Prius out of my way, I back my own car out of the driveway, somehow managing to calmly drive off down the road instead of backing straight into his bumper.

Against my better judgement, I look back one more time in my rearview mirror, just in time to see Jakub pull his stupid little car back into my driveway as if he belongs there.

Asshole. Asshole, asshole, asshole.

The mantra repeats in my head even as I trudge into my office. I keep my head down as I weave through the desks to my own, only raising my thermos in hello and making eye contact with a couple of other designers. They might have all gotten here early to attempt to keep up with our over-the-top workload, but I refuse. Bartholomew has made it clear that knocking out more projects won't increase our raise for next year, so I don't see the point in doing more.

The first thing I do is check my email, and the second thing I do is wish I hadn't. There's already a message from a difficult client asking for yet more changes on a graphic. And another from a different client asking for me to build out graphics for a series of programs, but giving me only the vaguest information that doesn't offer much in terms of what she wants me to do.

This day started out stupid and is shaping up to be a real disaster. All I can do is take a long pull from my coffee as I attempt to find a way to say *You're a terrible client and you're ruining my life* without actually saying it.

However, by the time a third client asks for something they clearly stated they didn't want before, I decide it's time for an upgrade from at-home drip to real coffee. Difficult people require quality caffeine. And a break.

"Coffee run," I mouth to Walter as I slip out the door. I'd offer to grab him one, but then he wouldn't get to escape the office for a while later today. We started at AdX around the same time and agreed early on in Bartholomew's tenure as manager that allowing each other a break from work was nicer than bringing back coffee for each other. Especially as the workload increases and the benefits of being employed here seem to dwindle, we have to make our own perks.

The only good thing about my job currently is that Drizzle & Drip is right down the block. It's quirky, artsy, community-focused, and most importantly, it's where Rafe works. He doesn't work on Mondays, but it's still a relief to step through the doors and feel a moment of peace. When I get back to the office, I'll have my boss breathing down my neck and micromanaging me, but for this moment, all I have to do is place my order and wait.

Even though I know it won't be Rafe at the counter, I'm still a little disappointed not to see him. I always look forward to chatting with him during my coffee runs, and today is no different even though I'm pissed at him for sticking me with Jakub.

Once I order, I move to the cozy floral print chairs by the front window to watch passersby as I wait. Normally I'd stand up at the counter and make small talk with whoever is working, even if it's not Rafe, but the café is more crowded than normal today and I don't want to be in the way.

I close my eyes and lean my head back against the chair, letting the smell of coffee and the feeling of not being at work wash over me. I've been on edge for the last couple days, between the bout on Saturday, nerves about Rafe moving in, and now anger and frustration that Jakub moved in instead.

After a moment, the hint of a familiar voice weaves through the din of coffee preparation, and my eyes pop open. I lean forward, trying to see the counter around the group of people waiting for their drinks. Finally, the crowd shifts, and there he is, looking sexy as usual.

"Sera?" Rafe calls out, holding up my miel in a to-go cup. When he sees me stand up, he comes out from behind the counter and walks toward me like a coffee-bearing Prince Charming.

My fingers brush against his woodworking-calloused ones as I accept my cup, sending a little zing of pleasure up my arm.

"I didn't think you were working today," I say, then wonder if memorizing his barista schedule comes across as a little stalkery.

If it does, he doesn't seem bothered. "I have to go to see my wood guy today, so I figured I'd stop in for a coffee, keep me alert for the drive," he says. "Saw your order come up when I went back to make my drink, so figured I'd make yours too since I know exactly how you like it. Are you heading straight back to work?"

"No, I have a little time." I don't really, but I'm not about to admit that when I have an opportunity for one-on-one time with Rafe. Work can wait.

He nods a little as he gets comfortable in the chair across from me by the window. "I wanted to tell you again how nice your house looked yesterday. I didn't see much of it, but what I saw was fantastic."

A stab of irritation courses through me at the mention of the disaster that was yesterday, but I push it aside. I don't know how to bring it up with him, but getting mad isn't it. "Next time you come by, we'll have to rectify that. Get you the whole tour." *Make you regret not moving in yourself*, I add silently.

"I also wanted to thank you for letting Jakub move in last minute like you did." Rafe takes the lid off his own coffee cup to blow on the surface. "I would have let him crash on my sofa for longer, but I think he needed a space of his own to really feel like he's settling back into the city."

"Totally," I lie, pursing my lips against the desire to ask him why the hell he let me think *he* was the one moving in. Because I really don't think he meant to deceive me. I've thought back through that conversation at the party so many times. There were moments where he may have been about to tell me he wasn't asking for him, and I cut him off so he didn't have the chance. And I never made it clear that I thought he was talking about himself. Really, it was a big stupid communication issue, and I can't hold that against him.

Much.

I am curious though, what brought Jakub back to the city. If he's going to try to take another job opportunity from me, I'd better be prepared. I'm about to ask when Rafe speaks again.

"That's why I like you so much. You always show up to support your friends."

Why I like you so much. Rafe likes me? So much? I mean, I knew he didn't *dislike* me, but I've always sort of suspected I'm never really on his radar. I hide my smile with a sip of my miel—which is, of course, perfect. Rafe always does the best job on my drinks.

I decide not to bring up my frustration with the Jakub situation. After his admission, I don't want to have to tell him that I'd only been helpful because I thought it was him moving in. I want to let him keep having a rosy picture of me as good and kind and selfless.

Which I am. Sometimes. When my least favorite person ever isn't moving in across the hall from me in my own house.

"I should get going. But tell you what," he says, standing, "you'd said you're still redoing your basement.

Next time I come by, let's look at the space and I'll make you a coffee table or something."

"Oh, you don't have to do that." I say it out of polite reflex, but I would actually love a table from Rafe. Not only is he a skilled woodworker, but it'd be a way to ensure I have more opportunities to see him outside of the café and team parties. Measuring the space, choosing wood, discussing styles. All time spent just the two of us.

Rafe lifts a hand to stem my refusal. "I insist. Call it a thank you gift for taking Jakub in on such short notice."

"Well, I appreciate it. Thank you." I appear composed and grateful on the outside, but inside I'm squealing with glee. Not only am I getting a bespoke piece for the house, but I'm going to get to spend more time with Rafe.

And if he is really such close friends with Jakub that he'd offer me a table just for letting Jakub move in, maybe they're close enough that he'll come over regularly. Movie nights. Game nights. Dinner. Naked sleepovers in my bed. You know, normal friend things.

Rafe flashes a grin and waves as he opens the café door to leave. "Have a good one, Sera."

I watch him walk around the corner to his truck and drive away before standing up myself and heading back to work. It was good to see Rafe, but now I'm thinking about the fact that Jakub and whatever one-night stand he brought over last night are currently at my house unsupervised. I'd bet money that he's snooping in my things, at least the ones in the common areas of the house. I make a mental note to go through all the rooms and clear them of anything I don't want him getting his grubby little job-stealing hands on. Just because I let him into my house doesn't mean I have to let him weasel his way into my life.

Chapter Four

Practice ran late, but I managed to get a lot of my anger at Jakub out on the track. It's not the first time I've done that. My ever-present frustration with Jakub and his job-stealing tendencies is the whole reason I joined the team to begin with. I needed an outlet for my pent-up rage, and derby is great for getting it out.

Normally when I come home, my house is dark and quiet and so peaceful, but tonight as I pull into the driveway behind Jakub's Prius, I look up to see lights on inside. A lot of lights.

So not only is he making himself at home in my driveway, he's clearly treating the inside like he owns the place too, not even caring about the electrical bill. *My* electrical bill. Because *I* own the house.

I'm ready to stomp inside and give him a piece of my mind, but my muscles are so sore from tonight's practice that the best I can do is hobble up the driveway. I need to get inside and take a hot bath so I can actually exist as a functional human tomorrow, even if I won't look much like one with how battered I am from taking hits all night.

Although I kind of don't mind the patchwork of colors on my skin from all the different stages of bruising. It makes a sort of watercolor-looking backdrop for all my tattoos, which is sort of cool.

Lifting each leg to walk up the steps of my front porch is a challenge in and of itself. As soon as I step through the door and glance at the stairs up to the second floor, I curse Past Sera for not choosing the tiny closet of a bedroom on the first floor instead of the big one all the way upstairs. Past Sera could have at least kept the pull-out sofa in the living room instead of sticking it in the basement. There's no place to sleep in this house that doesn't require stairs.

I pause as I close the door behind me. Something is wrong, and it takes me a moment to figure out what it is.

Where are my plants?

The living room had a couple of cute little plants on various surfaces this morning when I went to work. What the fuck has that asshole been up to all day? Just going through my house and disturbing or destroying everything I designed?

I drag myself through the living room into the kitchen, noting every change Jakub made while I was at work. I don't see where he hid my plants. I am going to rip him a new one when I get upstairs.

But first, wine. Thank fuck I left a bottle of pinot grigio chilling in the fridge. I had been planning on using it last night to toast Rafe's moving in, but now I'm glad I didn't end up opening it yesterday. I pour myself a generous serving in one of my vintage art deco stemless glasses, watching the play of colors between the glass and the wine, and take a large sip before setting the bottle back in the fridge.

I flick off every single light that Jakub carelessly left on as I shuffle back through the living room to the stairs. My muscles protest with each step.

Halfway up the stairs, I hear Jakub's voice floats down from his bedroom. "You're so beautiful. Did you know that you're beautiful?"

Does Jakub have a woman in his room again? Unbelievable. I wonder if it's the same one or a different one.

"Look at you, you're so perfect," he croons to her.

Ew. Gross, gross, gross. I nearly gag as I turn around and head straight back to the kitchen for the bottle. If I have to hear another word from Jakub flattering whoever he has with him, I'm going to need the rest of this wine. I may regret it in the morning, but not as much as I'll regret being sober while having to listen to Jakub getting it on across the hall from me.

At least I don't hear anything else from behind his closed bedroom door as I shut myself into mine. I've never been more grateful for my en suite bathroom. I'll be safe from having to interact with him and whoever the flavor of the night is tonight.

No, tonight I'm going to soak my aching muscles and relax and pretend that he's not here and my house is still completely my own.

I sip my wine as the tub fills with the hottest water possible. When the bubbles are high enough that they threaten to overflow, I sink down into the tub, hissing as the hot water scalds my skin. The first minute of these post-workout baths always hurts, but the heat will help my muscles relax after the tough practice I had. And the bubbles, they're just nice. They smell good, and combined with the chilled wine, they make the bath feel like a decadent treat instead of something that might boil me alive.

The first glass goes down easily so I pour another, snagging my phone off the little table next to the tub after I set the bottle back on it. Dialing Daphne, I put the phone on speaker and slide it back onto the table as I slip deeper into the water. I close my eyes and try to let go of all the stressors of the day—my boss, clients, the fact that Rowan is pushing us hard at practice.

And Jakub. Fucking Jakub.

"What are you doing?" I ask as soon as Daphne answers.

"Working on a puzzle," she says, her voice coming in and out as if she's searching the table for a piece and not directing her voice to the phone. "Why?"

"Want to hear something ridiculous?" I sip my wine and run my fingers through the bubbles, knowing she won't be able to resist the pull of gossip.

"Are you about to tell me how wonderful it is living with Rafe and all your dreams are coming true?" she asks, her tone dry. "Are we hearing wedding bells already?"

Daphne doesn't sound at all excited, which kind of stings. If her speculations were true, she should be excited for me. But I push the irritation aside, groaning and sinking deeper into the tub until the bubbles tickle my chin.

"I wish. Ugh, I'm so pissed. You'll never believe what happened." I launch into the story of Rafe's pseudo-betrayal.

"Are you kidding me? What the hell?" At least she sounds properly outraged, so I decide to ignore her lack of enthusiasm from before. "You're going to kick him out, right? You're not just going to let him live with you."

"It's not like I have a lot of choices here. If I kick him out, Rafe will think I'm the sort of person who doesn't keep their promises, which will not exactly endear me to him," I point out. "And even if it doesn't make him think I'm an asshole, he went out of his way to find Jakub a place to live. He'll never ask me for a favor ever again."

"Maybe that wouldn't be such a bad thing," Daphne tells me. "He wasn't exactly forthcoming with the details of this one. You really want to end up in the same sort of situation again?"

Even though I also wish he'd made it clear he was looking for Jakub and not for himself, I jump to Rafe's defense. "He may have been trying to. I just assumed it was him and didn't really give him a chance to clarify, but I also didn't make it clear to him that I thought it was him. We're both at fault for this."

She makes a noncommittal noise. "So, what, you're just going to live with Jakub? For how long?" Daphne's incredulity is practically tangible.

"I don't know," I moan. "But know what makes it even worse? I have to hear every time he brings a girl home." I gather up bubbles in my palm and consider face-planting into the foam, but opt for another sip of wine instead.

"What do you mean?"

"He has a girl in his room, literally as we speak. I heard him flattering her through his door." Even saying the words brings back the horror of that moment. I drop my voice an octave and mimic him. *"You're so beautiful. Do you know how beautiful you are?"*

"Yikes, that sounds like more punishment for you doing something nice," Daphne says.

"Who would go out with an asshole like him?" Do women in this town not see how awful he is? "He's a job-stealing asshole who probably hasn't even started unpacking his room yet."

Even though he found time to rearrange my decorations and plants downstairs.

"Maybe you should try being a really bad roommate," she suggests. "Just make things really unpleasant for him and maybe he'll move out on his own."

I consider this plan. "That's not a terrible idea, but I'd have to make sure to be a bad roommate in a way that wouldn't put someone else off from wanting to live with me at some point." Guy friendships might be different from girl friendships. I'm not sure how much Rafe and Jakub tell each other. I don't need stories of me being slovenly or putting a padlock on the fridge getting back to Rafe if I have any hope of potentially dating him in the future.

"If Jakub is such a playboy, maybe try ruining his one-night stands," Daphne proposes. "Maybe if these women see he has a sexy roommate, they'll all be either intimidated by you or scared that he's already sleeping with you."

"Gross, can you even imagine?" I make a gagging sound as Daphne laughs over the phone.

Even the thought of me sleeping with Jakub has me reaching for the bottle of wine to top off my glass.

"Why is there water splashing?" asks Daphne. "Wait, are you calling me while you're in the bath again?"

"It's convenient." This isn't the first time we've had this conversation. But I'm already sitting here relaxing. I might as well pair it with another task to make my time more productive.

Daphne sighs. "No, it's weird. Go put on clothes and then if you still want to chat, call me."

"Fine. Good night." I hang up and soak for a few more minutes before I climb out of the tub and wrap up in my fluffiest towel. My legs already feel better from the hot water.

Once I'm in pajamas, I climb into bed and debate reading for a little while before opening up the notes app on my phone. My time would be better spent thinking of a plan to torture Jakub than trying to focus on a book when all I can think about is how much this living situation sucks. Daphne will be up for hours still working on her puzzle. I'll make a list of a few good options and call her to narrow it down.

Chapter Five

When my alarm goes off the next morning, I grope for the phone and turn it off. I feel like shit. My entire body is sore from the hits I took at practice last night. The hot bath helped, but the wine didn't do me any favors. I roll my tongue around my mouth to try to disperse the dry, cottony feeling. It's gross.

I'm dozing again when my second alarm—the one that tells me I absolutely need to get up now—goes off, and I groan. I don't want to go to work, but I just bought a house, so I have bills to pay. I'll need to talk to Jakub about that. He should be paying half of all the bills. Once that happens, maybe I can get ahead on my mortgage or something. Although really, I should make him pay all of the utility bills for the inconvenience of having to live with him.

My annoyance at his continued existence gives me enough energy to roll out of bed and pull on my robe. I need coffee if I'm going to make it to work. Like an entire carafe of coffee.

I really should invest in one of those coffee machines with a built-in timer so it's already made and ready for me by the time I wake up. I can practically smell the delicious aroma wafting up the stairs now.

I shuffle into the kitchen and stop short.

Jakub is leaning against my kitchen counter wearing black boxers and a white T-shirt, sipping coffee like he's lived here his whole life. What the hell? He just moved in, he isn't allowed to be comfortable enough to walk around in his underwear, brewing my coffee and drinking it like it's his.

Jakub stares at me as he lifts the mug to his lips, and I suddenly remember that I'm standing in the kitchen doorway in my bathrobe. Which is not tied very well, and is therefore probably showing off my tiny sleep shorts and tank top. I quickly tug the robe closed. Jakub's eyebrows pop up as I tie the belt tighter around my waist, and I'm afraid that in my haste to cover myself I might have given him the impression that I'm naked underneath it. Gross. I do not want to think about him thinking about me naked.

Stomping forward, I throw open the cupboard that houses my mugs, feeling a surge of disappointment that he's just far enough way that he doesn't get hit. How is he so close as to be crowding me, but not close enough to at least have to duck out of the way of the cabinet door?

I squint at the contents of the cupboard, but I don't see my favorite mug anywhere. I know I washed it yesterday and put it back in here.

Oh, no. Don't tell me—

My eyes lock on Jakub, still watching me as he casually lifts my "I couldn't kern less" mug, with its letters all running together in a way that I find hilarious even though it's kind of a niche joke, to his lips.

After a moment in which I am proud to say I do not reach out and snatch the mug away from him, I grab my second favorite mug, the one that says "Photoshop Hero" next to a cartoon woman in a cape.

I set the mug down a little harder on the counter than I mean to, but luckily it doesn't break. The coffee pot is so far away. If I move close enough to get to it easily, I'll basically have to press up against him. There's plenty of room in this kitchen, and yet he's insisting on standing right here?

I reach awkwardly past him for the coffee pot, and as soon as I've poured myself a cup and returned the carafe to its place, I move to lean against the other counter. *It's not a retreat*, I tell myself, gritting my teeth. *It's self-preservation.*

Even though he should be the one moving. It's my house, it's my coffee, and it's only polite to move out of the way when you're blocking someone from getting to something. But Jakub Lattner isn't known for doing the right thing around me, so I guess I shouldn't be surprised.

"Making yourself comfortable, I see," I say, asserting my dominance so he doesn't think he's going to maintain the upper hand.

"I live here now, right?" He crosses his feet as he leans back against the counter, completely comfortable and casual.

I take a sip of coffee to give myself a moment to generate a response, then stare into the cup, confused Why does the coffee this morning taste better than usual? Is Jakub a wonder-barista as well as a job thief? Surely not. It's probably just due to my hangover and has absolutely nothing to do with his coffee-brewing skills.

"Only for right now." I go in for a second sip, thinking that surely the first sip being that delicious could be a fluke.

It's not. And I hate him even more for it.

"Oh, really?" He tilts his head and smirks. "You planning something to scare me out of living here?"

He's staring at me like he knows something. Surely he doesn't, though. Right?

I set my mug down with a heavy clink. "I have to get ready for work."

I'm sick of looking at his stupid face, reminding me that I'm going to have to be a lot more creative with how I make his life here hell if I don't want him to catch on. I stalk out of the kitchen and through the living room.

The door to the kitchen swings open, but I refuse to look back at him. He doesn't deserve my attention.

"The walls are thin," he calls. "Might want to be quieter when plotting diabolical schemes to get rid of me if you don't want me to know what you're doing."

Shit. He didn't just guess, he overheard me talking to Daphne? And if he overheard that, what else might he overhear through the walls?

Hell, if he can hear me, what am *I* going to have to overhear if he keeps bringing girls home?

I'm so caught off guard by this realization that I can't even come up with a decent response. But as I cross the living room, I'm reminded of something. "Move my plants back to where they were!" I call over my shoulder. He doesn't deserve niceties like *please* and *thank you* after his eavesdropping. "Where did you even put them? They were getting optimum light, and now you're killing them!"

"No."

He says it so calmly, with no heat at all, that against my better judgement I glance back at him as I turn to go up the stairs. He's casually standing just inside the living room, sipping his coffee as if we're having a friendly tête-a-tête.

"Asshole!" It's not the most clever response, but it's all I can muster. I stomp up the stairs and into my bedroom.

"It's nice to know you think about me when you're naked, though," he calls after me.

I slam my bedroom door, adding *immature* to *not clever* in the list of bad behaviors he brings out in me, and get dressed in a huff. This is not the way I wanted to start my morning. Why couldn't I have woken up to discover that the whole disaster of Jakub moving in was just a nightmare, and now that I'm awake it's all over?

As I fasten the clasp on my bra, I realize that I left my coffee downstairs on the counter. Great. I can't even have caffeine to soothe my irritation as I get ready to go into work.

Overall, I'm in a very bad, very grumpy mood as I finally open my bedroom door to leave. And it's just my luck that he's coming up the stairs at the same time I'm trying to go down. Well, he may have helped himself to my coffee and moved my plants and listened in on my private phone calls, but he doesn't get to take over the stairs. I stand my ground, refusing to move out of his way.

Unfortunately, he doesn't give way either. All I can imagine is hip-checking him the way I would an opponent on the flat track. He'd go tumbling all the way to the bottom of the steps, where he would land in a heap. Then I'd step right over his body and swan on out the front door.

I don't though. Because while it's allowed, even encouraged, in a bout, this is the real world and I do not need a lawsuit, which he would definitely bring against me because that's the type of person he is. Knowing him, he'd then hold that over my head for the rest of my life, while still refusing to move out and leaving me stuck with him as a roommate indefinitely.

So instead of shoving him down the stairs I say, "I feel sorry for the girl in your room. I just hope she gains the common sense to run away from you."

"Fuck you!" he growls, moving up a step closer to me.

"No, fuck you!" I take advantage of his movement to

shove past him, careful not to exert too much force while still jostling him enough that his coffee spills all over his shirt. When I reach the front door, I slam it behind me so the sparkly charm hanging on the other side of the door window bounces a little, making a tinkling sound against the glass.

Fuck. I still don't have my coffee.

The only thing that's going my way this morning is that I don't have to go back inside and get him to move his car. While I could use the opportunity to get my coffee from the kitchen, it would really undo any power I gained from our last exchange. I can't help imagining the scenario though, and playing through it in my head has me hunched over my steering wheel fuming as I navigate the roads to work.

Stomping into the office, I'm hyperaware of the fact that I'm not holding my usual thermos of coffee from home to help me get through the morning. I'm dreading opening up my inbox to find it filled with annoying requests from clients who think they know what they want, but really don't.

My mood must show on my face because when Walter sees me coming up the hall, his own expression shifts to one of mild alarm and he ducks into Tracy's office. As I pass it, I hear him say, "...looks like she's out for blood, I was afraid she'd body-check me if I didn't get out of the way."

I'll have to apologize at some point probably, but right now I'm still spiraling about Jakub eavesdropping on my convo with Daphne. And that comment he made as I left the kitchen. *"It's nice to know you think about me when you're naked."* Like I'd ever think about him while I'm naked. Gross. I mean, okay, fine, technically I was naked, but bathing is not the same as what he was implying and I hate him for insinuating that it is.

The worst part is that if he heard me talking to Daphne

through the walls, then he almost certainly heard me busting out my vibrator later to relax myself when I couldn't fall asleep.

So now that I'm paranoid about him hearing anything and everything through the walls, I'm going to have to either abstain from going solo or learn his schedule and take care of my needs when he's not home.

I plonk down into my desk chair and steel myself to open up my inbox. I guarantee all of my clients today are going to be nearly as annoying as Jakub, which is not going to do much for my mood, but I can't avoid them forever.

Chapter Six

I'm still grumpy by the time I get to the gym after work. I wish we had a regular roller derby practice tonight. I could really use the opportunity to take out all of this built-up annoyance on the track. But alas, I'm going to have to take it out on the treadmill instead.

I didn't even get any decent coffee today, having to suffer through the sludge at the office, because if I went to the café and Rafe was there...well, I'm not sure I would have been able to stop myself from telling him off.

Yesterday I had convinced myself that it was a miscommunication on both our parts. Today, I've pivoted and am just angry at him for not outright telling me he wasn't the one needing a place to stay. Sure, maybe I jumped to a conclusion, but he absolutely could have clarified at some point just to make sure I knew. He has to realize he wasn't clear about the fact that it would be Jakub moving in with me and not him. It was a very uncool bait and switch. Once I'm not so mad, maybe I'll suggest that he should make it up to me. Maybe with dinner. Followed by sex. Followed by falling madly in love with me.

Maybe even all of the above. If he feels really bad, I mean.

But for now, I'm going to take out some of this frustration on the treadmill. At least Daphne is joining me at the gym so I don't have to be annoyed and alone.

"You know these things can go faster than a leisurely stroll," I tell her as I set down my water bottle, phone, and towel on the stand for the treadmill next to hers.

"The treadmill does, but I do not," she says, carefully placing her bookmark in her historical romance and wedging it between her water bottle and the treadmill control panel.

"Yet you still come with me to the gym on my off nights." I pretend to look at her dreamily as I input my warmup speed. "You must really love me."

"Yeah, it's all about you," she says, her eyes roving over the other people working out.

My eyes follow hers and see two of my teammates benching weights in the corner by the mirror. Daphne can tell me she's here to be supportive of my working out and roller derby dreams all she wants, but the reality is that she's here hoping to see Rowan.

It's not a bad way to run into him since he does come sometimes, but even when he does, she never chats him up. Once I get rid of Jakub and have some time and energy to dedicate to it, I should definitely scheme a way to get him to stop his womanizing ways and get those two involved. There's no way I'm going to let him hook up with my bestie only to leave her in the middle of the night, which is his M.O. He doesn't even stay until morning. But once he realizes how great Daphne is, I have no doubt he'll stop that nonsense and treat her like a princess. He's a good guy, he's just never had a reason not to sleep around.

"Well, if we want to make this more about you," I say,

upping my speed on the treadmill, "I should warn you that you'll have to be careful what you say when I have you on speakerphone from now on, because Jakub overheard everything we said last night through the apparently paper-thin walls."

"This is why you shouldn't put me on speakerphone," she groans. "Especially not when you're taking a bath, it's just weird."

"I believe you mean practical and efficient," I correct her.

"Did he really hear everything?" I nod, and Daphne pauses to take a sip of her water, having to balance her book against the panel with her free hand so it doesn't fall to the conveyor and trip her. "At least we didn't say anything too awful or embarrassing. I can't imagine what he'd say if he found out I'm crushing on your team manager."

"I don't think he'll care." I squash the urge to roll my eyes. "Especially because he overheard our entire discussion about tricking him into moving out of my house."

"When would we even have time to plan out those pranks, let alone initiate them?" Daphne doesn't hold back her own eye roll. "That would never happen. It's just a dream."

"A delicious dream that I cling to," I say.

"Like your dream of dating Rafe?"

"Hey, that could happen. Especially because I have a new plan, which is to have Jakub invite Rafe over regularly. Which will be even better than living with him because this way he won't see my messy morning hair or anything like that, just the cute, adorable parts of me."

Daphne actually snorts at that. "After overhearing you plotting to convince him to move out, you think Jakub is going to do you a favor?"

She has a point. I'm not really in a position to ask him for anything at the moment.

"I have to do something," I counter. "I can't live with him getting comfortable in my house. This morning I woke up to him making a pot of *my* coffee, better than I make it because of course he's got to be better than me at everything, and then he drank it from my favorite mug without pants on."

"Wait? What?" The book falls as Daphne turns toward me and she immediately trips over it, sliding right off the treadmill and onto the floor.

"Are you okay?" I jump my feet to the sides of my own moving treadmill as I slow it down, but keep my eyes on Daphne.

"I'm fine." Daphne gingerly gets to her feet. She has a couple of scrapes on her hands, and looks a little shaky, but she climbs back onto her treadmill, waving in embarrassment at the other gymgoers who stopped what they were doing to make sure she was okay.

"Are you sure?" The first thing I learned when I started roller derby was how to fall properly, and that was more of a splat. "Maybe you should switch to the stationary bike?"

At least that would be harder for her to fall off. Not impossible, but less likely.

"I'm fine," she says again. In a hushed voice she adds, "So you walked into your kitchen to find him half-naked?"

"He wasn't half-naked," I correct her, frowning. "He had a T-shirt on, and boxers."

"Oh. You said 'without pants on' and I thought—never mind." She starts walking again, slowly. "Anyway, how are his legs? He looks like someone who has good legs," she says. "And it was morning, could you tell if he has good anything else?"

"Ew. I wasn't looking," I grind out. This is not the way I

imagined this going. She should be just as upset as I am, not talking about his morning wood.

"Even though you hate him," she says, "you have to admit he's gorgeous. With those dark soulful eyes, and the way he really looks at you when he talks to you."

"How do you even remember how he looks at you? He's been gone for over a year. You'd better not be developing a crush on him," I grumble, upping the speed on my treadmill again.

"I'm not," she says blithely. "But a hot naked man is a hot naked man."

"Again, he was not naked." I really need to stop saying the word *naked* with regards to Jakub. I shouldn't have had to say it even once, let alone this many times. "Besides, next to Rafe, Jakub doesn't even rank."

Daphne shakes her head as she sips her water, again holding her book so it doesn't fall. I wish she'd just put it on the ground or something so we don't risk a repeat wipeout.

"Seriously," I tell her, "you say Jakub is so 'soulful', but he never says anything serious. The whole world is a joke to him because everything always just works out for him. He doesn't even have to try. Rafe, on the other hand, is rugged and capable. His hands truly create art with his furniture, and he has the calluses to prove it." Just the thought of those rough hands gives me full body shivers.

"Yet he was still savvy enough to get you to let him move in with you," Daphne points out.

"It was a miscommunication," I grit out. "And at least I talk to my crush."

"And look how that turned out," she retorts, unfazed. "Besides, I talk to my crush. Occasionally."

"Oh? Did you finally talk to him after I left the party the other night?"

She nods. "We talked about that new bar opening up downtown at the last party."

"Did he talk to you about that, or did he talk to Tegan about the bar opening and you were standing next to them?" I feel like a jerk for pointing this out, but it's how things usually go for my poor shy bestie. Daphne needs to start getting realistic and either make an effort or move on.

"Maybe he was talking to both of us. Or wanted me to know it was opening so I'd go and he could run into me there," she throws out, refusing to look at me as she traces the treadmill buttons without pressing them.

"If you really want to spend time with him and interact with him," I say with a sigh, "you could join the roller derby team. Then he would be forced to spend time with you, realize how great you are, and fall in love with you, and you'll both live happily ever after." I silently add, *after he removes 'no derby girls' from his hookup rules.*

Daphne shakes her head. "We've talked about this. I love watching derby, but I don't want to play it. I'll stick to jigsaw puzzles. None of the pieces have ever hip-checked me."

"I love the violence," I say dreamily. "I imagine everyone on the other team is Jakub." It's completely true. Some of the hardest hits I've landed were all against him in my head.

"See? Like I said, violent," she sing-songs.

"Determined," I counter, upping my treadmill speed again now that I'm warmed up.

We have a big bout coming up and I'm determined to be ready. I'm not about to have the Rain City Rippers get the better of us, especially after Jakub got the better of me this morning.

He left the foyer light on again.

He's got to go. He can stay until he finds a new place, but he needs to start looking yesterday.

My workout took a lot out of me and I'm in desperate need of a snack, so I make my way to the kitchen. I should probably start carrying a granola bar in my gym bag or purse so I can eat on the way home and not be ready to gnaw the arm off the sofa when I get inside.

At least Jakub hasn't eaten my bananas.

I slice one up, drop a dollop of peanut butter on the edge of the plate next to it, and use one of the banana slices to scrape the remainder off the inside of the spoon. I'm about to pop it into my mouth when the door to the kitchen swings open.

For the briefest of moments, I think that I should have been faster with preparing my snack and sneaking upstairs to my room. But this is my house. I shouldn't have to sneak around or relegate myself to only one room just because I don't like my roommate.

Faking confidence, I slide the banana past my lips and slowly chew as I wash the peanut butter off the spoon without looking at Jakub.

"That looks good." Jakub snags one of the slices for himself, dipping it in my peanut butter.

This man has absolutely no boundaries! He's helped himself to my coffee and mugs, and now he's swiping food off my plate without even asking? That is not normal roommate behavior. That's not even normal friend behavior, until you reach a certain level—which he and I are definitely not at.

All I can do is stand there, mouth agape. I can't believe he did that right in front of me. Then he helps himself to a second piece and my outrage dissipates momentarily as I notice the flecks of soft blue paint on his fingers.

It reminds me of VanGogh's blue in his haystack painting. Or the comfortable blanket I have draped on the couch in the TV room.

But he's a graphic designer. We work on computers, not with paints. Is he painting a room in my house without my permission? It's a gorgeous color and would work great for a bedroom, but I mean, how inconsiderate can he be?

No way I'm going to give him the satisfaction of asking though. Instead, I dry my hands, a little rougher than I normally would, and pull my snack plate away from him.

"This is my snack, get your own."

"I've never had peanut butter and banana before," he says, casually opening the fridge and staring inside. "It's actually pretty good."

"I know. I'm the one who made it."

"Which is surprising because based on your fridge, I wouldn't say you spent much time in the kitchen." He grabs one of my sport drinks and opens it, leaning against the outside of the fridge.

"Just because I'm a woman doesn't mean I need to spend my time in the kitchen," I tell him. "Or were you offering to do all the cooking around here?"

No way is he going to agree to that. He dislikes me as much as I dislike him, I can't imagine he's offering to cook for me. Honestly, I don't even understand why he agreed to move in here when Rafe suggested it to him.

"Are you showing interest in my kitchen skills?" Jakub smirks at me from across the kitchen.

"No, I'm pointing out that you're being sexist."

"I don't mind cooking." He shrugs. "I don't love it, but it's not the worst. I can cook if that's what you want."

"I'm not asking you to cook for me." He'd probably try to poison me, or at the very least, spit in my food. "I'm merely trying to learn your weaknesses to get you out of my house." No reason to tiptoe around it. He listened in on my conversation with Daphne the other night so he already knows I want him out.

"Mm-hmm."

"But until then, we haven't talked about it but—you do know I'm not letting you live here for free, right?"

The look on his face says that I'm an idiot for even thinking that. "I didn't assume you were. I figured I'd be paying half the utilities and some kind of rent."

I'm a little surprised he doesn't fight me on it, but I'm not going to complain. With Rafe, I was willing to slow-roll that part, but I don't trust Jakub not to screw me over unless I've got it in writing. I'll have to see if I can find a generic lease template online or something.

"Okay. Good. I'll do up a lease agreement and leave it on the kitchen table in the next day or two for you to sign."

"Fine with me," he says, digging his phone out of his pocket as it begins to buzz. He swipes his thumb across the screen and holds it to his hear. "Hey, Rafe."

I'd been about to take my plate to my room to get away from Jakub, but at Rafe's name I stop and sit at my little eat-in kitchen table instead. If Jakub can eavesdrop on my conversations, I should be allowed to listen to his. If he doesn't want me to, he can leave.

Jakub smirks and turns to lean against the fridge again so I can see his face as he talks to Rafe. Not that I know what they're talking about; I can't hear Rafe's side of the conversation from here and I'm pretty sure Jakub is specifically trying to be as obscure with what he says to Rafe as possible just because he can sense my curiosity.

What an asshole.

"All right, see you then," he says, hanging up and sliding his phone back into his pocket as he strolls out of the kitchen.

"Inviting friends over?" I call, sliding my empty plate into the sink instead of washing it. Normally I wouldn't walk away without cleaning it, but this is an important exception.

"You showing more interest in me, Archer?" asks Jakub, standing in the middle of the living room as he turns on the TV. "Careful, I might start thinking you want to be my friend."

"I absolutely do not." Yet I find myself unwilling to walk up the stairs and leave Jakub to whatever he's doing.

"Well, I'll make sure to not get the wrong idea then, from your following me around the house." Jakub plops down in the chair, flipping through channels.

"I'm not following you around," I argue, sitting on the sofa. "This is my house and I can go wherever I want in it."

"And you're listening in on my phone calls?" he asks, not looking my way.

"You were literally standing two feet away," I counter. "Besides, you listened in on mine with Daphne."

"You talk louder when you're drinking, so it was almost impossible not to overhear every word."

"Fuck off." I'm not going to get anything out of this conversation. Standing, I walk around his chair and cross to the stairs.

"Does this mean you're not going to stay and watch the game with me and Rafe?" Jakub turns in the chair to look over his shoulder at me.

I freeze, my hand on the railing. If Rafe is coming over, I

do want to take the opportunity to spend time with him. However, I don't want Jakub to realize I'm into Rafe. He'd certainly find a way to use it against me.

"Ah-ha. Now I see," says Jakub with a little chuckle. "You have a crush on my best friend and want to use me to get closer to him."

"Or maybe I was already planning to watch the game. I just need to change out of my gym clothes." I stomp up the stairs.

It bugs me that Jakub has guessed my true motivation so easily. Even if I did think that the only benefit of Jakub being here is that Rafe might come around regularly, I don't want him knowing that that's my plan.

Not to mention, Jakub will be there with us hanging out. Ugh. Even if I didn't hate him, that wouldn't really put Rafe in the mindset of snuggling on the couch.

Upstairs, I strip off my sweaty gym leggings and tank top and jump into the shower for the fastest body wash I've ever done. I probably don't have time to wash the sweat from my hair, so after I towel off I take it out of its ponytail and blast it with some citrus-scented dry shampoo, fluffing it a little as I return to my bedroom to pick out an outfit that's cute, but not too much for hanging out at home.

I peruse my closet and select a pair of skinny jeans and a matcha-colored long-sleeved top. The tight pants aren't exactly comfy for a night of hanging at home, they do make my legs look good. And the shirt is loose enough to not look like I'm trying, but the deep V-neck still gives a slight hint of cleavage. Cute, but casual. I don't want Rafe to think I'm dressing up for him.

Especially because Jakub would call me out immediately and that would be embarrassing. He's already clocked that I'm interested in Rafe, and soon I'm going to have to slink back downstairs casually as if that's not exactly why I'm there.

I hear the front door open, and voices quietly chatting. I can't make out what they're saying, though, so I crack my door slightly and strain to listen. Jakub is probably intentionally talking quieter so that I can't listen in on them, not because he cares if I hear them talking but because he knows it'll bug me if I can't.

But then there are footsteps on the stairs, and I quickly and gently close my bedroom door so Jakub won't realize I'm actively trying to listen in. I keep my ear pressed against the door to hear everything I can though.

"Why, hello there, cutie," says Rafe.

The fuck?

Is he talking to Jakub? Surely that woman I heard Jakub talking to last night isn't still in his room. His door has been closed every time I've walked by, so I guess it's possible. I haven't even been able to see if he's unpacked or how he's set up the room.

"This is it here," says Jakub.

It sounds like he's having a completely different conversation. Is he ignoring whoever's in there? And why haven't I heard a single peep out of her?

"Gorgeous lines," says Rafe.

What the hell are they talking about?

Pressed against my closed bedroom door, I weigh my options. I could slip out of my bedroom while they're distracted and beat them downstairs. But what if they stay in Jakub's room for hours instead of going back downstairs to watch whatever game Jakub was hinting at earlier? I don't want to channel-surf all evening and miss out on the chance to just lay in bed and read.

Plus, it would be just my luck that as soon as I open my door, they will too, and that'll be awkward.

"Thanks," says Jakub. His voice is louder so he must be coming back into the hallway. "It's starting to really shape up into something."

"Maybe it's all the local motivation you're getting." There's a hint of a chuckle in Rafe's voice, and I wonder again what it is they're talking about.

"Yeah, yeah. I don't know if I should thank you or stop talking to you." Jakub's voice gets softer as I hear them walk downstairs.

Then the TV gets louder, and I can imagine them settling in to watch the game.

I count to sixty slowly, take a deep breath, and step out of my bedroom. I treat each step down the hallway as if I'm in a wedding processional because I don't want to rush, no matter how much I'm ready to be downstairs sitting next to Rafe on the sofa.

I picture it as I make my way down the stairs. Our knees will brush, and I'll feel the heat of his body against mine as we settle in. Maybe I'll make some popcorn and we'll reach for it at the same time, our fingers tangling in the bowl.

If just imagining it is this delicious, I can't wait to feel the real thing.

Chapter Seven

As soon as I reach the bottom of the stairs, Rafe smiles over to me with warmth. He smells like warm wood, comforting and cozy, and I subtly press my nose against his solid chest and breathe deep when he stands and wraps me in a hug.

"It's good to see you," says Rafe into my hair before letting me go and settling back into the chair.

"So glad you were able to come down and join us." Jakub smirks from where he's lounging on the sofa.

I roll my eyes. Jakub was the one who invited Rafe over, not me. I'm just taking advantage of an existing situation.

"We're watching the game, if you want to join us." Rafe snags a local craft-brewed beer off the coffee table and takes a sip. He must have brought it with him. I didn't buy it, and if the way Jakub is helping himself to everything of mine, I'm guessing he hasn't gone to the store yet.

Now it's Jakub's turn to roll his eyes. "I doubt she wants to watch the hockey game with us."

I can't decide if he's signaling to me that he'd rather I leave, or if he's being sexist again, insinuating that I don't know anything about sports and don't enjoy them. Either way, I'm not letting him win. I slide past his legs and sit down right next to him on the sofa.

"I'd love to," I tell Rafe. "Thank you." Too bad Rafe is in the chair so I'm stuck sharing the sofa with Jakub. I turn to my roommate. "I bet I know more about sports than you." No way am I letting him think I'm not as sporty as him just because I'm a woman.

"Do you even know how many of our college years were spent in a bar watching sports?"

"Do you know how many of my exes dragged me to bars to watch a game?" I counter.

"I used to watch Monday night football with my dad every week," says Jakub, stretching his arm along the back of the sofa as he turns slightly toward me in his seat.

"Same, and I used to attend every game of every sport my three older brothers played. Which was a lot of sports. Including hockey."

He gestures at the television. "If you really liked watching sports, you'd have a bigger TV so you didn't miss any of the action."

"And ruin the room aesthetic? How can you call yourself a graphic designer if you don't understand anything about balance and negative space?"

"You're definitely right about the negative space now that you're here." Jakub reaches forward to snag his beer from the coffee table, never breaking eye contact with me. He's issuing a new challenge. No longer are we playing *Who Knows More About Sports?* The game is now *Will Sera Rein It In or Show Rafe What a Bitch She Can Be?*

Before I can decide how to respond, Rafe jumps in.

"I haven't seen the basement yet, but you said you're going to make it into more of a family room-type space, right? I bet you could design it around a bigger television. I could even help if you want," he offers. "I mean, you did get my best friend off my sofa and into a real bedroom, so it's the least I can do."

"Thanks for the offer, but I don't watch TV much, so I don't think I really need a larger one." Plus a better TV might make Jakub more comfortable here when I'm already waiting for him to leave. Not that I'm going to say that in front of Rafe.

"Good point. You don't want anyone to think you're too approachable or average," says Jakub. He spreads out on the sofa, taking up more space and encroaching on mine.

Ugh, he's always in my space. My classes, my job interviews, my house. No way am I also going to give him the whole sofa, too.

I pull my feet up onto the sofa, forcing Jakub to either move or endure my socked feet pressing against his thigh.

"I mean, you said it was unfinished down there so you could really turn it into anything," says Rafe, apparently oblivious to the battle for space happening on the sofa.

"I suppose it would be cool to have a designated craft space, instead of having to get everything out and put it away all the time." Maybe it wouldn't be the worst idea to move up my timeline for finishing the basement. Jakub isn't budging, so I push my feet against his surprisingly solid thighs to move him more to his side of the sofa.

"There's no natural light down there though, right? So it should be an activity more suited for a dark space," counters Jakub, grabbing my feet with one hand and squeezing to stop my efforts to make him move.

"I suppose I could turn it into a dungeon for people who annoy me." I try to tug out of his hold without calling too much of Rafe's attention to it.

"I mean, both of those things are options," says Rafe, sounding unsure. He glances away from the game just in time to see me yank my foot away only for Jakub to pin it down again before I can kick him. "We could get together and look at the layout and diagram some possibilities."

"Didn't you come downstairs for something in the kitchen? Like a snack or a drink?" Jakub squeezes my foot harder, and I stop struggling for the moment lest he let go right as I'm pulling away so that I knee myself in the face or something.

I glare at him. "No, I had a snack earlier, remember? I'm good here."

Besides, has he seen Rafe? Rafe's a perfect snack. A lumberjack snack. Who should switch spots with Jakub.

"You could also turn the basement into a home gym," Rafe suggests, apparently deciding to ignore us fighting for dominance of the sofa. "Then you wouldn't have to keep paying your gym membership, and it would be more convenient."

I mull this over. "I don't know. I suppose it could be nice in winter, but I like going to the gym with the team. Nothing says 'team bonding' like burpees and dead lifts."

"What team? Like your coworkers? You're doing dead lifts with a bunch of graphic designers?" Jakub chuckles, seemingly entertained by the idea.

Rafe and I both stare at him, confused.

"Sera is a Tea City Roller," says Rafe. Now it's Jakub's turn to look lost, so Rafe adds, "The roller derby team."

"So you roller skate in short shorts and fishnets?" Jakub's eyes slide to mine, but his smirk doesn't feel like he's being mean, for a change.

It feels like he's...maybe kind if into the idea of me in short shorts and fishnets? Suddenly his thumb drags over the bottom of my foot and my stomach flips. Which is unsettling. I don't want flippy-stomach feelings around Jakub. It must be an instinctual reaction to having a guy touch me in an often-untouched place while looking at me like he might be kind of thinking I'm hot, but still. I shove the flip and all thoughts associated with it away.

"You mean, am I a tough, badass athlete on skates?" I raise an eyebrow at him pointedly. "Then yes, I am."

"And the team looks to be in good shape for the bout this weekend," says Rafe. His eyes are darting between me and Jakub and the way my foot is practically in Jakub's lap and he's holding it like he's about to give me a foot massage.

I'm suddenly very aware of the way Jakub and I are sitting on the sofa. Oh fuck, does this look like we're into each other? Does Rafe think that I'm interested in Jakub? No, no, no. I have to undo that. I'd tug my feet out of Jakub's hold if it wouldn't make it look like I'm pulling away because we've been caught doing something we shouldn't. Instead, I fix Jakub with the sternest glare I can muster and shove at his leg again. *See, Rafe? I'm just trying to get him to let me have some space on my own sofa. Because I do not want him in my space. You, on the other hand...*

"Yeah, I'm a little nervous with the number of jams they'll have me in," I tell Rafe. "But Tegan's been great at testing out my blocking abilities, and I think I'm ready."

"Well, you know I'll be there then to support the team. They made a great decision by moving you off the bench. You're a great blocker, and you're ready for the jams. It's the right thing to do." Rafe nods as he sets down his drink.

"How long have you been doing this derby thing?" Jakub asks me, but his eyes are directed at Rafe.

I start to count back to when I joined the team, but then decide I don't need to give specifics. "A year or so."

"Huh." Jakub sets down his own beer. "So, right around when I moved away then."

"A little before that, but year." He was at team parties with Rafe after I joined, does he seriously not remember me being there when I was the one of us who had a reason to be?

"Your art is coming along well though," says Rafe to Jakub, awkwardly changing the subject. Maybe he doesn't want to talk about derby anymore, or maybe there's a reason he wants to avoid the topic of Jakub's move. Whatever the reason, it doesn't matter to me. "That piece upstairs is gorgeous."

My eyes drop to where Jakub's hand is still resting on my feet, and the little flecks of paint on his fingers.

"Have you seen the painting yet, Sera?" asks Rafe, then turns back to Jakub. "Or are you keeping Lucy sequestered? I notice she hasn't taken over the house yet. But you let me in, so I figured..."

Who the fuck is Lucy? I pull my feet out of Jakub's hold, dropping them back to the floor and scooting as far away from him as possible. I'm about to voice the question when Jakub answers Rafe.

"I've just been letting Lucy get acclimated one space at a time, and removing possible toxins in the house."

"Who, exactly, is Lucy?" I ask.

Rafe turns to Jakub. "Dude."

Jakub's eyes flash to me. "I suppose I could go up and give her the option to come down." He stands and makes for the stairs, glancing between me and Rafe before disappearing up them.

This is the moment I've waited for. To be alone with Rafe. But I'm distracted by Jakub and whoever this Lucy is, so I can't even enjoy it. My eyes follow Jakub up the stairs until he disappears, and I sit for an awkward beat, staring at the empty stairs, before mentally shaking myself and turning my attention to Rafe.

I slide over into Jakub's spot on the sofa so I'm closer to

Rafe's chair, then lean my chin on my fist and give him my best flirty smile.

"What does your competition schedule look like this year?" I ask him. "I'd love to see you compete again." *Translation: I'd love to come check out the way your muscles ripple beneath your flannel shirt as you slam your axe into huge pieces of wood again and again.*

Rafe leans forward in his chair, putting our faces much closer together. "I have one coming up later this month, but it's a little ways out of town. Luckily they have some little cabins nearby, since it won't be feasible to drive back and forth for both days."

"Do you have someone going with you, or are you going on your own?" *Because I wouldn't mind crashing in a little cabin with you. Helping you stay on task. Handling your equipment. All your equipment.* I force my face to remain neutral and not betray the thoughts racing through my brain at the idea of being alone with Rafe in a little cabin in the woods, carefully checking over everything he uses for wood splitting. His axe. His gloves. His body.

Footsteps pounding down the stairs stop Rafe from answering.

"Well, I've opened my bedroom door, so we'll see if she decides to grace us with her presence," Jakub announces.

Of course he has to come back right as Rafe is about to tell me how lonely he would be in the cabin, and he wishes he could have someone to come keep him company. Jakub ruins everything.

He freezes as he enters the living room and sees that I'm in his spot, and Rafe is leaning forward, putting our lips mere inches from each other.

His eyes dart between us, and he sounds annoyed when he says, "I closed your bedroom door, Sera. I didn't know if you'd want Lucy in there or not." He clears his throat as he slides past my legs and sits down in the seat I'd abandoned.

He's sitting way closer than before, and I can't see if it's because of the way I'm sitting now or if he's actively left empty space on the other side of him. Now instead of just my feet touching his leg, his thigh is practically pressed against mine.

"I was just telling Sera about my competition at the end of the month, and how I'll be gone the whole weekend, and possibly part of the week as well," says Rafe, sitting back in his chair. Guess he didn't want to stay in kissing range with Jakub third-wheeling over my shoulder. Can't really say I blame him.

No, I blame Jakub.

"Oh, cool," says Jakub, reaching for his beer on the corner of the coffee table. He's all but lying in my lap with the maneuver, and I allow myself one brief, blissful moment to imagine standing up and knocking him to the floor. "Do you want me to come with?"

That motherfucker! First he practically lays on top of me for his stupid craft beer, and now he's stealing my potential romantic weekend away with the man of my dreams.

"Sweet. Thank you." Rafe's eyes flash between me and Jakub as takes a gulp of his beer.

"What are friends for," says Jakub, fixing his gaze on the TV. I'd forgotten the game was even on.

There's a beep, and Rafe digs in his jeans pocket to pull out his phone.

"I gotta get going." Rafe types out a quick reply before standing and sliding his phone back in his pocket. "We should catch another game soon."

"Definitely." Jakub stands and steps over my legs again

to clasp Rafe's hand between their chests as they slap each other's backs in a bro hug.

As soon as they part, I pop up and wrap both arms around Rafe. He's just so solid and smells so good. There is no way I was going to miss out on a chance to be held in his arms, even if it's only for a brief sweet moment and not a long spicy one.

When I reluctantly step back though, I bump into Jakub, whose palm presses against my lower back to stop me from backing up into him any farther. It's an intimate touch, even though I know he's only trying to stop me from knocking his beer out of his hand, and my stomach does that stupid flippy thing again. I quickly move away. His hand falls from my back, and as soon as Rafe steps toward the front door, I follow.

Right now I need as much space as possible between Jakub and myself. It's obviously been far too long since I've had a man's hands on me, if *Jakub* touching me is giving me butterflies.

I wave from the doorway as Rafe gets into his truck and drives away.

It's only once I've closed and locked the front door that I turn to find Jakub only a couple of feet away from me, leaning against the newel post for the stairs. His face is full of disgust.

"You couldn't make your intentions more obvious if you tried." He crosses his arms, tipping his chin toward the door in case I didn't realize he was talking about my feelings Rafe.

"In my experience, men aren't great with subtlety, so it's best to make my intentions very clear." I cross my own arms and narrow my eyes right back at him. I can't help it if men are dense and I need to beat them over the head with clues to get them to do something.

"Trust me." Jakub laughs as he drops his arms, but there's no humor in it. "If a guy wants something from you, he'll act on it."

He turns to go up the stairs, but pauses on the first step. "And now you want to come out? You didn't want to join us earlier, when Rafe was here?"

I peek around Jakub's shoulder and there on the stairs is the fluffiest white cat I've ever seen. And its bright blue eyes are shooting daggers at me. I've never felt so judged and insignificant in my life.

Jakub starts to head up the stairs, but stops and looks back over his shoulder at me when I splutter, "*This* is Lucy? Lucy's a cat?"

How the hell did he get a whole-ass cat in here without me knowing about it?

There's that asshole smirk again. "Who did you think Lucy was?"

"I had no idea Lucy even existed until thirty minutes ago. You didn't think to tell me you had a cat? What if I was allergic?"

He tilts his head, considering this. "Are you allergic?"

"No, but that's not the point!"

"If you're not allergic, then I don't see an issue." He starts up the stairs again, clearly over the conversation.

"The issue is that you can't just move into someone's house with an animal and not tell them! That's the kind of thing you have to clear with everyone else living there before you move in."

"Well, I'm telling you now." He bends to scratch the cat's head, and she leans into his touch. I can hear her purring from the bottom of the stairs. "I have a cat. Her name's Lucy. I had to move your plants so she doesn't eat them and get poisoned."

I point at him, latching on to that. "See? That! That

right there is a reason to warn me that you had a cat. Because if you had asked me to move the plants so she doesn't eat them and die, I would have! I'm not a cat murderer."

"Glad to hear it."

"But you didn't ask! You just moved in with a cat, put all my plants god knows where, and what, expected I'd be chill about it?" The cat's tail twitches, and I swear if she had fingers she'd be showing me the middle one.

"They're at Rafe's. And trust me," Jakub says without looking back, not a trace of emotion in his voice. "I never expect you to be chill about anything." He disappears up the stairs, and Lucy and I watch him go.

"Can you believe the nerve of this man?" I ask the cat when he's gone. Clearly she can believe it, because she just stares me down, tail twitching rhythmically.

Lucy obviously gets her bitchy attitude from her dad. He didn't even bother to properly introduce us. Such an asshole.

I've never had pets, and my only real experience with cats is the cranky old man my grandmother had when I was little. I tried to pet him once and he hissed and scratched me, and I've given cats a wide berth since then. What if she also doesn't like me? Or tries to swipe at me as I go past? The least he could have done was observe as I held out a hand for her to sniff, to make sure she didn't try to bite me or anything. Because right now she looks like she wants to murder me.

Putting off crossing paths with Jakub's judgmental cat for a bit, I turn away from the stairs and go into the kitchen. The banana was a while ago, and I worked out hard enough that I'm hungry again. I grab a handful of blueberries and make my way warily back to the stairs.

Thankfully, Lucy is gone. I bounce up the stairs,

popping blueberries in my mouth, and am in the hallway when my phone's incoming text tone goes off. I pause outside of Jakub's partially open door to check the message.

It's from Daphne. *Heads up. Bad weather coming through tonight.*

I groan. Bad weather is not what I need right now. *Thanks,* I text back, then immediately pull up the weather radar. Not that I need to double-check Daphne—she wouldn't warn me unless it was true—but I want to see it for myself. Sure enough, there's a huge storm system moving our way.

My anxiety is already ramping up. I hate storms. Thunder, heavy winds, lightning, all of it. I always have. This is exactly why I insisted on buying a house with a basement.

I have a little bit of time, but the storm could speed up and get here at any moment so I race around my room, changing into comfortable sleep clothes, brushing my teeth, and grabbing my pillow and some sheets and blankets. No way do I want the storm to start while I'm still upstairs. Then I'll have to go through the house to get to safety while the weather rages on the other side of the very thin, very breakable windows. Nope, I'm going right to the basement and I'm sleeping down there so I'll be safe no matter what.

"What's going on?" Jakub yanks his door open all the way as I hurry past to the stairs.

I glance down to see that Lucy is also peeking out around the wall to eye me. I'm sure I look harried, but right now Jakub is not my biggest concern.

"There's going to be a big storm coming through." I flash him the image of the weather radar that I still have pulled up on my screen.

"It's just a thunderstorm."

Flipping him off, I hurry down the stairs. I don't owe him an explanation. For one thing, he doesn't deserve that insight into my life, and for another, explaining it to him will take too long. I want to be safely ensconced in the basement *now*.

Although he doesn't say anything more, I hear him grumbling and an indignant meow before his footsteps trail me through the living room and kitchen, then down into the basement.

The basement is just a cement floor and cement walls, not at all cozy, but much safer. And I planned ahead for this exact scenario when I moved in, buying a pull-out sofa knowing I'd be sleeping down here sometimes.

I balance the cushions against the side of the sofa and grab the cord to pull out the mattress. It's not a top of the line sofa bed, but the reviews said it was decent. Besides, I'll only be down here when there is a storm, and I have all the other house payments so I wasn't looking to spend a fortune on it.

As soon as I have the mattress pulled out and the legs secured, Jakub, clad in a pair of black sweatpants and a light blue T-shirt, tosses his pillow down on one side. My side.

"So we're sleeping here tonight, then?" says Jakub, glancing around the basement with distaste.

I get that the room is bland as hell and not remotely inviting, but even if I agree with him that it needs some work, I'm not going to let him insult what I own.

"No, I'm sleeping down here." I toss his black pillow to the concrete floor and begin spreading out the white fitted sheet I brought down.

"Great," he says, taking the other side of the sheet and tucking it in. "Like I said then, we're sleeping down here tonight."

"You said 'it's just a thunderstorm,' so if you're so unbothered, you can go back upstairs and sleep in your own bed." I flick out the pastel pink top sheet with more force than is warranted, but I'm angry. He's invaded my house and my personal space, and acted like he thinks I'm being silly for worrying about the storm, and now he's coming for my safety space too. Not cool.

"If it's bad enough that you're sleeping in the basement," he says, gently smoothing the top sheet and spreading it over the bed and tucking in the bottom, "there's no way I'm subjecting Lucy to that when it's an easy choice to keep her safe."

"You brought your cat down with you?" I try to sound annoyed when I say it, but if I'm being honest, I think it's sweet that he takes such good care of his cat.

"Of course. I'm not going to leave her upstairs if there's a chance it's unsafe." He gives me a look that's very reminiscent of the one his cat had given me on the stairs earlier. Like he's disgusted with my stupidity.

"Fine then. If you insist on sleeping down here"—I throw one of the two deep green blankets on the ground next to his pillow—"then you can sleep on the floor. I'm not sharing the bed with you."

"You're joking, right? It's a cement floor."

"So sleep on the cushions. I don't care."

"That would still be terrible for my back." Jakub picks up the blanket I tossed at him and spreads it out on the bed. "Besides, there wouldn't be enough room on the cushions for both me and Lucy."

"You sleep with your cat?" *This is not cute, this is not cute.* If I say it enough times, it will become true.

He must mistake my surprise for derision, because he snaps, "Of course I sleep with my cat!" Jakub grabs the second blanket out of my hand and shakes it out so it covers the whole bed on top of the other one. "What, you think I make her sleep on the floor? She's my cuddle buddy."

I stand there staring at him, surprised. If Rafe had told me he cuddles with a cat at night or that they had a bedtime routine, I would simply melt. But hearing that asshole Jakub does this? I'm not sure what to feel.

Finally, my brain turns back on, and I shake my head to clear it. "Doesn't she need a litter box or something?"

Maybe she's been trained to hold it overnight, I don't know. I've never had a pet before, and, except for my grandma's old cat, I've never been around them at all. I'm pretty sure watching funny cat videos on the internet doesn't count.

"There's one in the corner." Jakub nods his head to the far corner of the room as he climbs into his side of the bed, which at least is now the other side from where I prefer to sleep. "I put it down here so she'd have an extra one when she decides she wants free run of the house."

Seriously? Is there not a single room in my house that he hasn't taken over? I'm annoyed that I can't even fight him on it. I'm not a horrible person and can't make an argument against the safety or comfort of an innocent animal, even if that animal does seem to hate me.

I'm never getting my house plants back.

"This mattress is the worst. I hope you didn't pay money for this," complains Jakub, shifting from side to side to get comfortable.

"At least I own more than a room's worth of furniture." It's not a great comeback, especially because as I climb under the blankets on my own side, I realize he's right. This bed sucks.

"If I'm paying half the bills, then this sofa is half mine, at least while I'm living here." Jakub lays on his back with his phone in the air.

I can't see what he's doing on it, but I refuse to give in to his bait. Flipping onto my side to keep my back to him, I grab my own phone off the armrest and let Daphne know that I'm safe in the basement and that I wish she was also in a basement somewhere. Then I switch over to watching the weather radar. The storm is getting closer.

Pleased with your pull-out sofa? she texts back.

I switch back over to our text thread.

It's not amazing, and it's even worse now that Jakub is sharing it, I text back. I can hear him punching his thumbs against his screen. How does one type so loudly on a touchscreen?

You're in bed with Jakub? Daphne responds, then adds a string of laughing emojis.

This is not funny. I did not invite him to sleep in the basement with me. And he brought his cat. In between each text, I pop back over to the radar to note any changes so I can mentally prepare myself.

He has a cat? she asks.

Apparently. I just found out tonight. Can you believe he didn't tell me that?

No, but I mostly can't believe you're sharing a bed. First you see him naked, and now you jump into bed with him, she texts. *If I didn't know any better, I'd assume you're crushing on him.*

Nope, absolutely not, I type back, but my mind immediately jumps to the solid feel of his thigh when I was pressed against him upstairs on the sofa earlier. I shove the thought away.

Doesn't mean you can't snuggle up to him. Daphne

adds a winky face. *Aren't you always telling me to consider other men until my crush takes notice of me?*

Luckily, I'm safe from that. He is already planning on cuddling his cat. I add my own string of laughing faces.

Sounds like he knows how to take care of a pussy then. This is followed by one of those stupid kissy emojis.

I'm not even going to respond to that. She's obviously been drinking or something. I don't want the words *Jakub* and *pussy* in a sentence together anywhere near me. Which is a shame, because the joke would have been hilarious if it was about anyone else.

I check the time. Eleven p.m. The storm still isn't here, and I need to get up for work in the morning. I turn up the volume on my phone in case of an emergency weather alert and set it on the armrest.

Peeking over my shoulder as I adjust the blankets, I see that Jakub is still playing on his phone. I guess if he isn't going to give up and go back upstairs, I'm going to have to live with this. Better than being up in my room during a storm, at least.

Even if he is the last guy on Earth I would choose to share a bed with for a night.

Chapter Eight

Boom!

I jolt awake. The room is dark, and then there's a flash of white by my head as something jumps onto the armrest and stares down at me.

I would scream if I had any air in my lungs, but all I can do is whimper and scramble backward, away from the gargoyle leering down at me.

Arms wrap around me, pulling me tight against a warm, solid body.

Who the hell is in my bed?

I'm about to scream and kick out at the person when there's another big boom of thunder, and my fear of the gargoyle and of the person holding me against him is forgotten, overrun by an even more visceral terror.

I look wildly around, my eyes beginning to adjust to the faint hint of light let in by the tiny glass block windows up by the basement ceiling. My gaze lands on the monster on the armrest.

It's not a gargoyle. It's Lucy. And the way she's glaring at me, I think the gargoyle might actually be the less scary option.

Now I'm stuck between a cat that looks like she wants to eat my face off, and the person who I finally remember is Jakub. I've got nowhere to go, and panic begins to claw its way up my throat.

There's another loud burst of thunder, and my pulse ratchets up. I didn't know my heart could beat this hard and fast. It feels like it wants out of my chest, and to hide anywhere that could be safer than this basement.

"It's okay," murmurs Jakub, rubbing his hand along my forearm. "I'm right here."

He's trying to soothe me, but it's having the opposite effect. I don't want him to be right here. I'd rather literally anyone other than him be right here. And I really hate that he now knows about my fear of thunderstorms. He's sure to use it against me somehow.

Even worse, when the next thunder booms, I curl myself into a ball, pressing back against him, and it's clear that this little fear-based cuddle fest is having a definitive effect on his body.

Either that, or he's sleeping with a soda can in his sweatpants.

The next flash of lightning makes me jump, prepping for the sudden boom that will arrive any moment. I shift on the mattress to clamp my hands over my ears as the thunder shakes the walls.

Jakub's sharp intake of breath near my ear, and the way he quickly drops his hand from my arm to my hip to hold me still, distracts me the tiniest bit from the knowledge that another thunderclap is bound to be barreling toward us. His hard length is wedged against my ass, and I bet he's trying to hold me still because he's hoping if I don't move, I won't notice, and he won't be embarrassed.

He's caused me so much stress these last few years, and now he's basically turning my life upside down by moving in uninvited. But now I've got something I can use against him. At the very least, he'll have to live with the knowledge that I know I made him hard. And maybe I can use that as leverage to ensure he doesn't find a way to use my fear of thunderstorms to embarrass me.

I shift my hips, rubbing against him. His corresponding groan is exactly what I was hoping for.

Finally, I have some power over him for once.

When I press against him again, his fingers tighten on my hips, his arousal still hard against my backside as he hisses out a breath. I'm debating my next move when another thunderclap shakes the world.

I startle, my attention pivoting from tormenting Jakub to the storm. To his credit, Jakub also stops moving. His hand slides from my hip to my shoulder.

"It's okay. You're okay," he whispers. The gentle circles his fingers are tracing on the skin exposed by my tank top are actually soothing this time, as long as I don't think about who they're coming from, and I start to relax a little.

Until he moves his hand from my shoulder and grazes my nipple through my sleep shirt.

I'm certain it was an accident. But accidental or not, my body responds involuntarily by gasping and arching into the touch, which presses my ass against his hips again.

We both freeze. His fingers are still millimeters from my breast, and if we weren't both wearing pajamas his erection would be wedged between my asscheeks. I think we're both waiting for the other person to make the next move, and since it's rarely me who gets to call the shots with Jakub, I don't want to waste the opportunity.

The one barely-there touch of his hand has my nipples crying out for more attention, but I remind myself that this is supposed to be about making sure he knows that I'm well aware of the embarrassing fact of his arousal. So instead of moving his hand back to my breast like I want to do, I focus on shifting my hips just enough to provide a bit of friction against him. He sucks in a breath, so I do it again.

One-upper that he is, Jakub responds by curling his fingers so they skim over my nipple again, and this time it's definitely no accident.

I roll my hips more deliberately, and his hand palms my breast over my shirt. Another hip roll, and he pinches my nipple. A zing of pleasure shoots straight down to my clit, and when I whimper, he does it again to the other nipple.

So that's how he wants to play it, huh? Oh, it's on.

Reaching behind me, I brush my hand over his hard-on, feeling a wet spot where he leaked pre-cum. His hips buck against my hand, and I close my fingers around his dick through the fabric of his pants. He groans, and I stroke him a few times before moving my hand away in silent acknowledgment that my turn has finished and it's his go again.

But instead of upping the ante again, Jakub lets go of my breast and catches my hand in his. He guides it back to his cock, pressing it against his length as he gently thrusts his hips against my palm where it's trapped between his shaft and his own hand.

Now this is interesting. Jakub Lattner, forfeiting his turn so I'll continue jerking him off?

He groans, letting go of my hand to slide his own across my hip and around to my front, cupping it between my legs over my sleep shorts. He pauses with it there, not moving except to continue his gentle thrusting into my hand, and the heat of his fingers so close to my core has me wet and aching in a matter of seconds.

The rules of the game seem to have changed, and I no longer know what they are, nor do I care. All I care about is that the fingers between my legs are writing a check that they'd better cash or I might lose my mind.

This time when I roll my hips, he rolls his too, the hand at my pussy moving to drape my leg over his to allow him better access. When his palm closes over me and those paint-flecked fingers find my clit through my sleep shorts, I bite my own lip to keep from crying out. I won't give him the satisfaction of knowing how good it feels.

A flash of lightning and I hide my face in my pillow. If I can't see anything, I can pretend this is just a dream. Fleeting like the storm that is somehow no longer at the forefront of my mind.

Jakub's breath is coming faster behind me, keeping time with the fingers circling my clit as we both race toward climax.

If I can get there first, I can still let go of his dick, roll over, and leave him desperately wanting something he almost got to have, just like he's done to me countless times over the years. I can snatch his orgasm from him like he's taken so many jobs from me.

I just have to beat him to the finish.

I loosen my grip on his cock slightly, but that just seems to provide him with more fabric-on-skin friction that, if his increasingly erratic thrusting is any indication, is actually helping speed him along. So I close my fingers tighter around him again, although at this point I'm not sure anything I do or don't do will make a difference.

And I'm close enough to my own orgasm that as long as he doesn't stop what he's doing, I don't think I care who comes first. I only care that I get to come at all.

When Jakub lets out a moan and stiffens behind me, and the fabric under my palm becomes suddenly damp as his cock pulses with his release, I barely even notice, so consumed am I by my own climax coursing through my body at the same moment. My hips thrust against his fingers and stars burst behind my eyelids as I come apart, stifling my cries of pleasure in my pillow.

We both remain still as the aftershocks radiate through us, chased by the implications of what we just did.

That was unexpected. Even though I'd initiated it, I'd only planned to tease him a bit and then call it all off.

There was nothing teasing about what just happened between us though. And the realization that Jakub—Jakub! —just gave me one of the best orgasms of my life without even moving a stitch of clothing out of the way is as terrifying as any boom of thunder I've ever heard.

Jakub bumps his nose against my shoulder blade. Or at least, I assume that's what he was doing. Surely he didn't just press a kiss to the tank top covering my back. Then he moves my leg from where he'd draped it over his and rolls to his side of the bed, turning his back to me.

I don't move. My clit is still pulsing in the aftermath of my climax, and the gusset of my underwear is soaked.

That's how I know it was real.

And it was all my doing. I'd initiated it. Never stopped it. Enjoyed it.

Not that I will ever let him know that.

What am I going to tell Daphne?

Nothing, that's what. She cannot know about this. She's already shipping me with Jakub, and this will only add fuel to that. This was a serious lapse in judgement. My defenses were down because of the storm, and I made a stupid decision that got out of hand. That's all.

I'm not sure what his excuse is, but that's not my problem.

I can hear him breathing softly on his pillow behind me. Another clap of thunder sounds, but it's so much quieter than it was that I barely even hear it. I realize that I don't remember the last time lightning flashed outside the tiny basement windows. The storm must be almost over, and I didn't even notice.

Finally, I shift back into a sleeping position, flipping the pillow over so my cheek isn't pressed against the faint ring of dampness where I'd stifled the moans of my orgasm. As I settle back down on the pillow, my gaze lands on Lucy, still perched on the arm of the sofa.

If she wasn't judging me before, she definitely is now. It's clear from the way she daintily steps off the armrest, one paw at a time, and onto the bed to walk to the corner farthest from me, where she curls up by Jakub's feet. She is not impressed with my behavior.

Same, kitty. Same.

I stare at my phone, willing the numbers on the clock to crawl forward. They refuse, so I check the weather radar again. Doesn't look like we'll have any more storms today.

My alarm won't go off for another hour and a half, but I turn it off and slide out from beneath the blankets, careful so as not to jostle the mattress too much. I can hear the steady rise and fall of Jakub's breath and know he's not waking up any time soon, but still.

I don't want to push my luck.

Sneaking up the stairs, I push open the door as slowly as possible, wincing when it creaks. I really need to oil the hinges.

Before I can close the door behind me, Lucy darts between my legs and through the kitchen, clearly on a mission to do whatever cats do this early in the morning after being shut up in a basement with two people who hate each other.

Although whatever that was between us in the wee hours didn't feel like hate.

I open up my texts as I make my way up to my bedroom. *Meet me at D&D in thirty*, I text Daphne, using our shorthand for Drizzle & Drip, but her notifications are silenced while she's sleeping, so she won't see it right away.

When I'm upstairs and have closed myself in my room, I text her again. *Let me know when you see this.* This time I hit 'notify anyway' and wait a beat to see if she replies. When she doesn't, I type, *Daphne I'm serious I really need to talk to you.* I take my phone into the bathroom with me, sending one more message. *Something happened last night and it's not an emergency-emergency or anything but I'm freaking out.*

Finally, little dots appear, indicating she's typing.

I'M AWAKE, she replies. *Café in 30. You're buying the coffee. And it better be a strong one if I'm dragging myself out of bed at this hour for a non-emergency freakout.*

That's fair. See you soon.

I wouldn't normally repeat-message at 5:30 a.m., but I need to process this and it would be way too complicated over text. I lay awake last night after Jakub fell back asleep, debating whether or not to tell Daphne even though I knew I was going to end up telling her. She's going to give me shit for it, but she's my best friend. There's no way I'm not going to tell her.

I rush through my morning routine as quickly and quietly as possible before slipping downstairs, shoes in my hand for extra sound prevention. I even manage to avoid Lucy.

I can't believe I'm doing a walk of shame out of my own house. Daphne is going to have a field day with this.

Pausing in front of the café, I pray to the coffee gods that Rafe isn't here this morning. This is the first time I've ever wished to not see him, but it would be just my luck that he'll be working an extra shift and overhear everything. Then thanks to the bro code or whatever rules guys have for situations like this, he'd report it all back to Jakub. I'm not sure if I still have any leverage over Jakub about last night given my...participation, but if I do, it'll be gone the second Rafe tells him what I'm about to tell Daphne.

However, I must have done something good in a previous life because Rafe isn't anywhere in sight.

Stepping up to the counter, I order an americano with an extra shot for Daphne, and a miel for me. Then I tack on a couple of bakery treats for good measure.

While I wait for my order to be ready, I settle into the coziest corner in the place. It's rarely open—a perk of being here so early, I guess—with the two floral chairs with a little circular coffee table between them. And it offers a perfect view of both the front door that Daphne will come through and the side door that Rafe will probably use if he shows up for some reason.

I really hope the universe decides to continue being kind to me. Even if Rafe doesn't overhear and report back to Jakub, the irony of having to watch him man the barista station while I tell Daphne all about how I let his best friend get me off last night.

And liked it.

But it was a one-time thing. I don't even like the guy, much less want a repeat of whatever that was, even if I did enjoy it. I'm going to have to tell him it was a mistake. That it can't happen again.

Ugh. That's going to be an embarrassing conversation.

The door opens and Daphne stomps in, looking

exhausted and very grumpy. She walks right past the barista and collapses in the chair across from me.

"You owe me a coffee," she grumbles.

"I have a miel and a double-shot americano on the counter for Sera," calls the barista.

"Coming right up." I shoot out of my chair and collect both drinks, bringing them over and setting them on our little coffee table.

Daphne raises an eyebrow as she watches me turn the cups so the handles are perfectly aligned.

"Two cream cheese danishes!" the barista calls out.

"Ope, that's us too." I hurry over to collect our little treats.

"You either want something from me, or you're about to tell me River left The Sympathy, which is it?" Daphne is looking more awake now. She eyes me with suspicion as I place the danishes on the table with the coffees.

"Don't worry, your favorite band is fine," I promise her, "And I don't want anything. Can't I just be an awesome friend who gets you a pastry because I want to?" I sit back down, focusing on taking the first sip of my miel instead of looking her in the eye. I want to tell her what happened, but I want to take the secret to my grave just as much.

"If you were truly an awesome friend, I would still be sleeping." Daphne rolls her eyes, but she still picks up her own coffee. "So what's this non-emergency that was such an emergency you had to text me at oh-dark-thirty?"

I set my cup back down in the saucer with a clink and sit up a little straighter, steeling myself. I'm a badass derby girl. I've got this.

"I slept with Jakub." It comes out in a rush. "Well, kind of. But it was an accident."

"On the pull-out sofa, I know. You told me."

"No." I grimace. She's really going to make me spell it

out. "I mean, yes, but also...we sort of fooled around. Accidentally."

"What the fuck?" Daphne blurts.

The barista looks over with a frown, and I wave her off and silently mouth, "*Sorry.*"

"At least you waited until I was done swallowing to drop that bomb." Daphne sets her own coffee cup back in the saucer with a clatter. "But seriously, what the fuck? I thought you hated him."

"And I do," I assure her.

"How do you accidentally fool around with someone? Especially someone you hate?" She rips off a piece of her danish and pops it in her mouth, then gives me a conspiratorial look and lowers her voice. "And how was it?"

My face is beet red, I just know it is. I glance around the café. There are a couple of people in suits waiting for their to-go coffees before work, but they're all on their phones and probably not listening in on our conversation. I fan my flushed face, which Daphne appears to take as an answer to her question, because she squeals and claps her hands.

"Okay, so you said it was an accident. How does one accidentally fool around with somebody? Did you get blackout drunk or something after you texted me?"

"It was the bad weather," I say. "And it's never going to happen again. I don't even know why I'm telling you. I knew you'd give me shit about it."

"How can it be the bad weather's fault? Did the storm startle you onto Jakub's dick?"

"You know how freaked out I get during thunderstorms, I wasn't in my right mind," I explain. "Besides, it never would have happened is he hadn't felt the need to join me downstairs for some reason, so it's his fault, not mine."

"Uh-huh. 'For some reason.' Like because of the bad weather that also drove you downstairs?" asks Daphne, completely deadpan. "Because it's safer in the basement. He probably saw that you were freaking out and figured if you were that worked up it must be a really serious storm, and he didn't want to be upstairs if the house blew away."

"Okay, fine, whatever." I wave a hand, dismissing her logic and rationality. They weren't invited to this conversation. "But he refused to sleep on the floor."

"The cold, hard cement floor," she says.

"So I had to share the bed, against my will," I continue, ignoring her. "And when the storm woke us up, he was just kind of comforting me and it happened. Spontaneously."

If by 'spontaneously' we mean 'I made a conscious decision to fuck with his head and it got out of hand.' Or, more accurately, it got very much in both our hands.

"Jakub comforted you? Are we talking about the same guy here? The one who seems to always be there when something good is about to happen to you, and then it happens to him instead, like he planned it? That Jakub?"

"Yeah. I was shocked too. And annoyed, at first. But he was actually really sincere about it. Which is weird."

"It's not that weird. He's always been nice to me. Although people are always around," Daphne says thoughtfully. "Whenever you're nearby though, he does come off as more critical."

"Exactly. Everyone is always 'Oh, Jakub is the best!' But he's never said a single nice thing about me or my work." Not that I need or necessarily want him to compliment me. But it's weird that I seem to be the only person he has nothing nice to say about.

"All right, back to the important information. How was it? Tell me everything." Daphne sips her coffee and leans toward me, all ears. "Nobody could have such nice hands as his and not be good in bed."

I'd thought that maybe her thinking I fanned myself

because of the fooling around would be enough and she'd let it go. I should have known better. I rip off a piece of my own danish and slowly chew to buy myself some time.

"Rafe has nice hands," I say, changing the subject.

"We're not talking about Rafe, we're talking about Jakub. Whose hands have already been all over you." Daphne pops another bite into her mouth with satisfaction. "And I want to hear exactly how good those hands are at what they do."

"I'm not sure you deserve this danish now." I tug her plate closer to me, but she knows I'm just teasing.

"Oh, don't be like that just because I'm telling you the truth." Daphne swipes my fingers away from her plate. "Are you really not going to give me anything? Not even whether or not it was good?"

I sigh, knowing she's just going to keep bugging me till I tell her. "It wasn't, like, full-on sex. We didn't even take our pants off." I tell her about realizing he was hard and thinking I could tease him a little, just so he knew that I knew, and then it turned into us taking turns teasing each other. "And then I tried to move my hand away and he held it there, and then put his on me, over my shorts, and the next thing I knew we were dry-humping and we both came in our pants."

"Wow." She sits back, taking it in. "So what happens now?"

"What do you mean?"

"At some point you have to go home, which means you have to see Jakub again," she says. "It's not like you can avoid him forever like you usually do."

We've been friends for so long, of course she knows my M.O. with guys.

"It was in the middle of the night. Maybe he thinks it

was just a dream." I wish I could do the same thing, but it's all seared into my memory.

"I wish I had those kind of dreams." Daphne laughs her rare full, big-presence laugh, drawing the attention of few people in the line and making me shush her. I hate to do it, because she's usually so controlled and quiet, but I'm already embarrassed enough without the other café-goers staring at us.

"All right, fine, I'll stop. You have to go to work anyway. Thank you for breakfast, coffee, the laugh, all the things." Daphne finishes off the last sip of her coffee and stands. "Have fun at work. Don't hurt anyone."

"Yeah, yeah." I pick up my own coffee to finish as Daphne blows a kiss and breezes out of the café, leaving me alone with the memory of Jakub's hands on me.

Chapter Nine

Later, at practice, I channel all my annoyance at my job into skating harder and faster. One of my clients today insisted they'd told me to use a different color scheme, but I'm positive they didn't. I have the email where they requested red and gold, but they insist that they changed to blue and gold and told me on the phone. I've never talked to them on the phone, so there's no possible way they told me verbally to change the colors, but my boss still made me scramble to change over all the assets right before the deadline.

At least I was too busy to think about Jakub and last night.

And right now, for practice, all I have to do is focus on the next play.

Our team manager blows the whistle and we take off, quickly forming a fireman line. It's not easy to match our rhythm and speed, but we make it work. That's the whole reason we practice it like this, so we'll be able to find it faster in an actual bout.

"Great, now break line and form the Gotham Web," Rowan calls. "Make sure all the lanes are filled."

We drop our hands from each other's hips and shift to

fill out the track, preventing a jammer from potentially getting through. We grab hands, and it feels like playing Red Rover as a kid.

"Now imagine a lead-jammer is trying to get through," yells Rowan. "Tegan, get in there."

As Tegan starts her jam, I wait for her to move into a play area. As soon as she does, I'm whipped forward. I imagine Tegan as a combination of Jakub and my annoying client as I hip-check her into the infield.

Tegan flies to the side, and Rowan blows his whistle in three quick bursts.

"That was a great booty block, Sera, but you're not actually trying to kill your teammates," he calls.

"Sorry!" I skate over to Tegan and hold out my hand to help her up.

"Let's just call it a night," says Rowan, twirling his finger to gesture around us. "Rest up for this weekend."

"Don't worry about it," Tegan tells me, brushing off her leggings. "Someone clearly did you wrong, and I wouldn't want to be that person right now."

"You have no idea." I laugh. It's either that, or start venting. I like my teammates, but I'm not ready to get *'I hooked up with my evil roommate'* levels of personal with them.

"Look, I'm grabbing a drink with Rowan after this," says Tegan, gesturing where Rowan is picking up some cones from our practice. "Want to come? You can vent, or just drink. Your choice."

With Rowan letting us out early, if I go home Jakub is bound to be awake still. I'm not ready to face him yet. I'm not sure I'll ever be.

"Yeah, that sounds good. Thanks." I'm not sure if I'll vent, even about work, but I could have a glass of wine. It won't be as good as drinking in my bathtub at home, but at least it's something.

The floor of the bar is sticky, and it's so dark in here I'm not sure the lights even work. It's about as dive-y as they come.

Tegan and Rowan seem to be regulars. We slide into a booth and before we have a chance to order, the bartender is already bringing over three bottles of beer. No glasses anywhere in sight. Beer isn't my drink of choice, but I doubt they even serve wine here.

"Thanks," Tegan tells the bartender, who tosses a weak salute as he returns to the bar. Tegan passes the bottles to us.

Rowan accepts his as he stretches out on his side of the booth, already looking around the bar. Probably scoping out potential women he could bring home for the night.

"You don't have to tell us what happened," says Tegan, grasping her beer with one hand and grabbing a piece of chalk off the table with the other. I look down and realize the table is actually a chalkboard. That's kind of cool. "We've all been there. Just make sure you use all that anger this weekend at the bout."

"The Rain City Rippers have a strong lineup, and they're going to spot a weakness to juke super quick," adds Rowan, turning his beer between a finger and thumb as he continues looking out at the crowd.

"Anyone in particular we should look out for?" Tegan is using her chalk to sketch out a pair of skates on the table.

I check my phone, trying to be subtle. No messages, and

still too early to go home for at least another hour. Jakub for sure won't have gone to sleep yet before then.

"Not this weekend, but for our next bout, yes," says Rowan, dismissing our current concern. "We'll do some recon on them after this upcoming bout."

"I'll be ready," says Tegan.

"Good." They're not looking at each other, barely interacting as they talk.

I've always wondered at their friendship. They've never dated or hooked up—Rowan only has one rule, and that's that he doesn't sleep with anyone on his team, and Tegan isn't interested in men. But they act like an old married couple, so they've obviously known each other a long time.

"Let me know when you're ready," says Tegan, putting in some shading.

"Will do."

"It's his turn for me to be his wingwoman," explains Tegan, not looking up from her drawing on the chalkboard table. "And then tomorrow, we'll go to a lesbian bar and he'll be my wingman."

"What a good friend." It's kind of cute that they take turns helping each other, even if it is for one-night stands.

"Except for the time the woman I was chatting up turned out to be bi, and went home with Tegan instead of me." Rowan finally glances our way, mock-glaring at Tegan.

"I said I was sorry," she says, but her grin betrays the truth.

"Who are you waiting to text you?" Rowan's gaze returns to the line at the bar.

"If they're not texting you, they don't want you," says Tegan, accepting a new beer from a passing bartender. "You should move on."

"It's nothing like that." I don't know if Jakub even has my number. Although I suppose he could get it from Rafe if he really wanted it. Not that I want him to text me. I'm actively avoiding him by not going home. But I find myself wondering if he's even noticed that I didn't come home after practice.

Although given that he didn't even know I'm a derby girl, it's unlikely he knows my practice schedule. Probably he just thinks I'm out doing something he'd deem boring or silly, like going to the bookstore where Daphne works or shoe shopping. I finish off my own beer and swap it out for a new one. If I'm going to sit here, I might as well drink. Maybe it'll distract me from what happens when I do finally go home tonight.

We sit in silence that I find a bit awkward but they seem to find companionable, Tegan coloring on the table and Rowan people-watching.

"All right," says Rowan, finally setting down his drink. "I found someone."

"Okay." Tegan sets down her piece of chalk. "Let's do this."

I check my phone as they slide out of the booth. It's not really late enough to go home, but maybe Jakub will have gone to bed early. I don't particularly want to stick around here to watch Tegan help Rowan pick up a woman, nor do I want to stick around here drinking alone, so I guess I don't really have any other option. Home it is.

Jakub's car is in the driveway, so he's almost certainly home. I doubt I'll get lucky enough for him to have walked to one of the places nearby or have been picked up by a friend.

He left the lamp on in the front hall again too.

Still racking up my electric bill. Not cool.

Although I suppose it is nice to come in the front door and not be in complete darkness. Not that I'm about to thank him for it. He probably wasn't even meaning it to be kind. I bet he wasn't even thinking and left it on out of negligence.

As I set my purse on the table next to the lamp, I can feel eyes on me. I turn to the stairs, and there sits Lucy. Judging me. Again.

I'm tired from practice and from barely sleeping last night, and I just want to go to my room, take a bath, and go to sleep. There's no avoiding the cat, but at least she's not Jakub.

I click on the flashlight app on my phone and turn off the lamp, slowly walking up the stairs past Lucy.

"Good kitty." It looks like Lucy is only going to watch me, not swipe out or anything. "Good kitty."

I get past the cat and up to the hallway. Jakub's door is slightly ajar, and it's pitch black in his room. I can hear him breathing softly. Good. I won't have to face him tonight.

I slip into my own room, closing the door so Lucy can't get in, and breathe a sigh of relief.

Chapter Ten

Daphne doesn't want to go out after the gym. I'm not surprised. She likes to go to bed early. But it doesn't stop me from trying to convince her.

When it becomes clear I'm not going to win, I try calling Tegan. No answer. She's probably already out at a bar with Rowan, taking her turn to hook up with someone. So unless I want to go someplace alone, I'm forced to go home early. Or at least, at my normal time.

I drive home with dread pooling in my stomach. As soon as I pull onto my street and catch sight of my driveway, my anxiety ratchets up.

Jakub's car isn't here. I can see through the sidelight window that the front hall light is on again, but other than that there are no signs that anyone might be home.

I park my car and let myself into the house, the sense of foreboding loosening its grip on me. There's a folded paper with my name written on it on the hall table, propped against the lamp.

'Out with Rafe. Don't wait up. - Jakub'

My shoulders relax for the first time since Jakub moved in, and I realize just how sore they are from the last week's worth of workouts and stress. Now I can fully relax, knowing that Jakub isn't home and won't be for a while. I guess he really doesn't have my number, or he probably would have texted me instead of leaving a note. It's kind of surprising that he bothered either way, but I appreciate the confirmation that I am once again alone in my house for the first time in days.

I turn off the lamp and race up the stairs to shower and change into my comfiest stay-at-home clothes before strolling confidently through the quiet house to the kitchen. It's snack time. Jakub isn't going to come in at any moment and steal bites of my banana, or drink my sports drinks, or put his snobby craft beers in my fridge.

Although as I slice up a banana, it occurs to me that while Jakub is out with Rafe, he could be telling him about last night. The thought makes my blood run cold. How will he spin it? Will he make it sound like he dreamed it? Like he's the one who initiated? Does he realize that I enjoyed it, and will he tell Rafe that?

Whatever he says, if Jakub tells Rafe, it will ruin any chance I have at dating him. But there's nothing I can do about it except hope that guys don't tell each other everything the way girls do.

I grab a handful of chocolates and set them on my plate next to the banana slices as I head into the living room for reality TV. I'm going to take advantage of this opportunity to watch whatever I want without judgement. No one needs to know I have a weakness for baking shows.

Lucy chirps her way down the stairs and sits across from me. So much for no one judging my TV preferences.

"I'm not sharing with you." I dip a piece of banana in peanut butter. Once I chew and swallow, I add, "No matter how much you beg."

She watches every bite make its way from the plate to my lips. It's unsettling, being stared at so unblinkingly.

I still have more left on the show when I run out of my snack, so I go into the kitchen for a glass of wine to really take advantage of there not being anyone around to have an opinion on what I do. When I return, Lucy is sitting in my seat. Just like her dad, taking over my space.

How did she get there? I didn't hear her move.

I can't just lift her out of the way. She'd probably scratch me if I tried. I weigh my options. I could sit in the chair, but the view of the TV is better from the sofa. Plus, this is my house, not the cat's. She can have the spot, but she can't have the entire sofa. So I sit at the other end, giving her plenty of space.

"Guess we're having a girls' night," I say to her. Maybe if I talk to her, she'll think I want to be friends and will decide to be cool with me. She offers me a slow blink, which I choose to take as agreement that this is a girls' night and not a threat to end me. "Baking TV and drinking. Too bad you can only participate in one of those things. I don't know anything about cats, but I'm pretty sure I shouldn't give you wine."

I turn my attention back to the TV. Every so often I glance her way, and I swear she's getting closer to me. She's not moving in a threatening manner, but I'm still a little nervous that she keeps creeping toward me. What if she's trying to lull me into a false sense of security?

I look over at the chair. I could just move there, view be damned, and then I wouldn't have to worry about her getting close enough to attack me, but I'm pretty sure I'm supposed to establish dominance with animals so they don't think they run things. With any luck, Lucy and her dad will be leaving soon, but in the meantime, I can't let her think she's the boss of me, so I hold my ground.

"You're not stealing another seat from me, cat," I tell her, my eyes trained on the television. "My butt is staying right here. This is my house and I'm in charge."

I feel a little better having verbalized my determination out loud, but it doesn't deter Lucy. In fact, by the time the show is over, she's stretched out against my thigh, still watching the TV as though she has a vested interest in whether or not the fruit pies will have a soggy bottom and how the judges feel about the crust crimping.

Her fur is so fluffy, like a cloud. Should I pet her? She's touching me of her own accord, but I don't want to try touching her and make her mad. I decide not to risk it, but my fingers itch to see if she's as soft as she looks.

I check the time. It's late, and Jakub still isn't home.

My thumb hovers over the button to play another episode. I'm enjoying feeling at peace in my own home again, and cuddling with Jakub's cat isn't the worst thing ever. It's actually kind of nice having her weight pressed against me. We could just stay here until she decides to move. Then I won't risk Lucy swiping out at me in anger for moving before she's ready.

But if Jakub comes home and I'm still down here, he might think I'm waiting up for him—either to talk to him, which I don't want to do, or because I'm worried about his safety, which I'm not. Frankly, I'd still like to avoid him, and the best way to do that is to not be somewhere where I'll have to see him when he gets home.

So I turn off the television and slowly inch away from Lucy, who turns her head toward me and makes a little *prrbt* sound as if she's a robot turning back on after being in sleep mode. I immediately freeze, waiting to see what she does. We've been sitting together quite calmly for at least half an hour, but who knows what mood she'll be in now that she's focused on me.

When Lucy just stares at me and doesn't hiss or swipe out with her claws, I continue to inch around her and into the kitchen to rinse my glass and put it in the dishwasher. As I walk through the living room again to head upstairs, I glance over at the sofa. There she still is, sitting there, just watching me. She almost looks as if she's trying to assess the situation.

Seeing no immediate threat, I continue past her to the stairs. The longer I linger, the higher the likelihood that Jakub walks in and catches me standing here as if I'm waiting for him.

Placing my foot on the first step, I pause and look over my shoulder at the lamp on the table, just inside the door. The one that Jakub has left on every night that I've been out. Without it on now, the entire first floor of the house is dark.

But I'm not his mom or his caretaker, and I don't need my electric bill to be higher, so I take another step up the stairs.

"*Meow*," Lucy calls. I swear I can hear the judgement in her voice.

There's no way she's asking me to turn the lamp on. And even if she was, I've decided to stand my ground with her so she doesn't think she can boss me around. I'm not caving to a cat. That would be ridiculous.

"*Meow*."

It's too dark to see her, but I can tell she hasn't moved from the sofa. Maybe she's not telling me to turn that light back on. Maybe she's telling me to come back and watch more TV with her.

"I'm going to bed. No more TV tonight."

"*Meow*."

That one sounded insistent. Not like she's disappointed that I said no, but like she really needs me to do something for her. She meows again, and I glance at the lamp. "Can't cats see in the dark? You don't need the lamp. And neither does your dad, he's got a flashlight on his phone if he needs light."

She's silent for a moment, and I think I've made my point. I turn again to go upstairs, and—

"*Meow.*"

Fuck me.

Tromping back down to the lamp, I flick it on, and glare at where Lucy sits on the arm of the sofa. "Fine, the stupid lamp is on now. Are you happy?"

I wait for Lucy to respond, but all she does is blink both eyes at me slowly. I can't believe I'm actually standing here talking to a cat and waiting for her to talk back. What am I doing?

I start back up the stairs, refusing to look behind me. I'm not a cat person, and she's Jakub's problem. Not mine.

Closing my bedroom door, I get ready for bed, but as I'm sliding between the sheets, I swear I hear scratching at the door. I pause and listen, and when it doesn't come again, I decide I probably misheard. I settle the blankets around me to get comfy and reach to switch off the light.

Scratch, scratch, scratch. It's definitely coming from my bedroom door. I didn't mishear it. And it's not stopping.

Tossing off the blanket, I huff over to the door. As soon as I crack it open, Lucy shoves her way inside my room.

"No, no, this is my bedroom. Your bedroom is over there." I open my bedroom door farther and point toward Jakub's bedroom door, which is definitely cracked open for her to be able to go in and out of her own free will.

Lucy ignores me. She leaps deftly up onto my bed and immediately starts kneading my duvet.

"You shouldn't get onto other people's beds without

their permission," I tell her. "You need to be in your own bed. Not mine."

Lucy simply curls up, not even facing me, and closes her eyes.

I'm too nervous to pick Lucy up and put her out of my room. Or to shove her off my bed. Who knows how she would react? "Fine. But when your dad gets home later, you need to move from my bed to his."

I leave the door slightly ajar for her to get out later, then climb back into bed very gently, making sure not to jostle the covers so I don't disturb Lucy. She's kind of in the middle more than on just one side, so I don't really have enough space.

Forced to lie on my side, I curl awkwardly so as not to upset the cat. It's not comfortable, but it's better than making her angry and getting scratched.

It's because of Lucy that I'm still awake when I hear the front door open a while later. I haven't been lying here listening for Jakub to come home safely. But the sound of his footsteps coming upstairs are the last thing I hear before I finally drift off.

The music is pumping out in the arena. I can't hear the lyrics, but the bass is already settling into my pulse as I try to keep my hand steady so my eyeliner doesn't go wonky. We're up against the Rain City Rippers tonight and I'm not confident we'll win. I'm not about to lose and have terrible makeup to boot.

The door to the locker room flies open. "Sorry! Sorry!" calls Tegan as she races inside.

I can see Rowan in the hall as the door swings shut behind her. "Where the hell have you been?" he yells.

"Derby girls are always late," Tegan says with a shrug, already shoving her bag into a locker.

"Get ready fast," Rowan shouts from the hallway. "They're announcing us in ten."

"Oooh, someone's in trouble with the boss," I tease as Tegan plops down on the little bench next to me.

"He'll get over it in five minutes." She rolls her eyes as she tugs on her fishnets. "I'll buy him a drink and he'll forget this ever happened."

I pause and look at her as I slide my pencil back into my makeup bag. "Isn't the party at his house tonight?"

"Even better." Tegan shoots me a grin. "I'll bring him one of his own drinks and won't be out any cash."

"Rollers! Let's go!" calls Rowan, cracking open the locker room door.

"See you out there." I toss my bag into my locker and skate out into the arena.

We all gather behind our sign, bouncing in place to keep our energy up. The music is a lot louder out here, but this is what we need. We're about to go out there and rock this place, so we need the game songs to motivate us and get our blood pumping.

The announcer begins to introduce the players, and we each skate out and wave to the crowd when he calls our derby names. As soon as I hear him say, "Matcha Mayhem!" I take off, skating a lap and letting the crowd see how badass I am. At work, they see me as a doormat who will do exactly what needs to be done even if it means totally changing the design, no matter how close to the deadline we are or how ridiculous the request is. But out here, I'm in charge. And I'm someone for the other team to contend with.

I feel confident as fuck, and want the crowd and the

other team to see it, but I can't help grinning as I spot Daphne in the crowd holding a glittery poster-board that says, "GO MATCHA MAYHEM!!". She's even wearing our team T-shirt. If we were the type of team to have a mascot, it'd definitely be Daphne. She never misses a game. Or a party.

I'm delighted to see that Rafe is next to her, his red flannel standing out in the crowd of mostly black. He'd mentioned he might come when he was over earlier this week, but I'm surprised he showed up. He made a plan and followed through, and that is so sexy.

I shoot him a wink and sashay my hips a little as I fly past him on the loop.

I'm riding the high of seeing my crush as I line up for the first jam of the night. As soon as the whistle blows, we pack up, determined to block out the other team's jammer. This is our night. And there's no way I want Rafe to see me open up a whip for their jammer and not Tegan.

We're holding off their jammer for a good lap, but then I make the mistake of glancing up into the crowd. I nearly trip over my own toe stop when I spot Jakub standing right beside Rafe and Daphne.

I don't look away fast enough, causing me to break the pack. The other team's jammer sneaks through and immediately taps her hips to call off the jam.

"What the hell?" shouts one of my teammates, bringing my attention back to the track.

Fuck me. I glare up at Jakub as we reset for the next jam. I can't believe I let him distract me.

"Rugby start," signals Rowan.

We get into position on the pivot line, and Bruise Brew whisper-yells, "Get your head in the game!" at me.

"Rule one," I whisper-yell back, reminding her of the

well-known derby rule of taking it easy on newer players when they make mistakes.

The ref blows the start whistle and we move into the scrum, bracing for the jammers to try to tussle their way through. We just have to last out the two minutes, taking the legal hits and hoping Tegan can earn a lap point to get us ahead. We're going to need the buffer with this team.

The ref blows the whistle again to end the bout, and we can finally release. I'll have some lovely new bruises later, but at least I didn't let my teammates down again.

The refs call a barcode meeting, so at least I have a moment to grab water and calm myself down a little. This is the first time I'm seeing Jakub since the basement, and the timing could not have been worse.

I don't mean to look back up to where he stands with Rafe and Daphne, but I can't help it, and I wonder if he's ever actually been to a roller derby match before. He's looking around like he's uncertain about where he is and what's going on.

I can't believe Rafe brought him. I suppose my hope to avoid him the rest of the time he's living in my house was a little unrealistic, but why did it have to be now?

The rest of the night I make a conscious effort to not look their way, even when I'm not actively playing. I'd love to see Rafe, and Daphne, but I absolutely do not need Jakub ruining my focus again. Although I'll admit that the knowledge that he's watching gives me an extra edge of aggression to push off harder for every block, and not a single jammer gets through me for the rest of the night. I simply imagine each and every one is Jakub, and knock them all down.

Chapter Eleven

My ponytail is still dripping down my back from the shower I raced through after clinching our win against the Rain City Rippers, but I can't be bothered to completely dry it. Not when Rafe is out here. Hopefully he hasn't left yet. I barely even take the time to swipe on some mascara and lipstick, but I want to look at least a little cute for him.

"Is he still here?" I ask Daphne when I find her by the flat track. I shift the weight of my skates tied over my shoulder as I look around the hall.

"Are you referring to Rafe or Jakub?" There's a teasing glimmer in Daphne's eye and I raise an eyebrow at her in pretend annoyance.

"Ha ha. Rafe, obviously." Although it would be nice to know if Jakub is also still here so I'm prepared for the awkwardness that's sure to happen when we see each other.

"They both went to check out the vendors," she tells me, but her attention is directed at Rowan, standing a little ways away chatting with Tegan and a few other people.

"Why don't you just go over and talk to him?" I ask her. "You could congratulate him on the game. After all, he was the one who called the plays even if we're the ones who flawlessly executed them."

"Flawless, huh? I saw you let that jammer through," she says, not taking her eyes off her crush.

"That one doesn't count," I grumble. Or at least, it shouldn't. It was all Jakub's fault. He's not supposed to be here, in my space. And after what happened between us the other night, anyone would get flustered seeing him out there if they were in my skates.

But Daphne's not even paying attention. "I'll just say hi to him at the party."

"Orrrr you could go over to say hi now, and then say hi again at the party." The best defense is a good offense. "Then you get to talk to him twice."

Daphne turns to say something, but I cut her off.

"Rafe's coming over." I stand up straighter, and barely manage to avoid wincing as my skates knock into my back, alerting me to the exact locations of some of my new bruises.

"And Jakub's right behind him." Daphne smirks. "I'll meet you at the party."

I grab for her, not wanting to have to face Jakub alone, but she slips away. I watch her walk out and notice Rowan has also left. She's probably trying to be one of the first guests at his house for the party to get some alone time with him, not that she'll use it to her advantage. My poor, sweet, shy Daphne. She won't be the only one trying to get there early to spend time with him, either. Already, some of his go-to groupies are starting to meander to the exit.

"You did awesome," says Rafe.

He throws his arms around me in a bear hug, and I immediately drop my gym bag to wrap my own arms around his waist. The weight of his arms presses the wheels of my skates harder against my blossoming bruises, but the pain is worth it.

"Seriously, great job out there," says Rafe, releasing me and stepping back. "That other team was tough."

"Thanks." My cheeks heat at his praise, even though he's completely accurate. I kicked ass out there, and that team was a challenge.

Jakub is hovering awkwardly right behind Rafe. I wish he would go stand anywhere else. Like maybe in the next state.

I decide to keep ignoring him. "What did you buy?" I ask Rafe. It's obviously a shirt, but I want to see which one he picked out.

"I've been eyeing the new team shirt for a while." Rafe holds it up in front of him. "And they finally had one in my size."

"Tegan did a great job on that design," I agree. I'm a little disappointed that it's not one of my jerseys, but at least he's still supporting me. I'm part of the team, so it still counts.

"Jakub got one too." Rafe gestures to Jakub, who waves it at me in an awkward hello.

"Cool." I'm not sure what else to say. I can't even look Jakub in the eye, especially not with my crush standing right here between us.

"So, where's Daphne?" Rafe looks around for her. "I wanted her opinion on something, uh, over there." He gestures vaguely to the vendors who are starting to tear down their booths for the night.

"She already headed out to the party at Rowan's." I wait for him to ask if he can get my opinion instead, but when he doesn't, I say, "Are you coming tonight?"

Rafe knows most of the team and he usually comes to these parties, so I'm not really asking so much as just filling the air so Jakub doesn't have a chance to say anything uncomfortable. Besides, if he says he is going, I can offer to walk out with him, and then we'll probably get there at the same time and can walk in together. It'll almost feel like we're going together-together, and I can't wait to see the jealous looks his groupies toss my way.

"You're going?" Rafe glances briefly over at Jakub, who stands there like a statue, inspecting the design on his new shirt very intently. If I didn't know better, I'd think he was feeling just as weird and unsure as I am.

"Of course, the whole team will be there."

"Uh, then, yeah, that sounds good. We could do that, right, Jakub?" Rafe reaches out and pulls Jakub up to his side. "He hasn't had a proper night out since he got back, it'll be good for him."

My eyes immediately cut to Jakub's. Did he tell Rafe what happened between us? Did he ruin my shot at happiness with his best friend just to be an asshole?

In a stage whisper, Rafe adds, "He's been super moody all week, won't say why. Probably to do with his stuffy ex."

Okay, so maybe he hasn't said anything. Good. My shoulders relax a bit. But when neither of them says anything, and I notice that Rafe is raising his eyebrows with his head tilted toward his friend, it becomes clear that he wants me to officially invite Jakub too. I don't want to, but if it gets Rafe there...

"Sure. Yeah. You should come too, Jakub." I don't bother trying to sound like I mean it, but Rafe claps Jakub on the shoulder like they've just been given the gold ticket they've been waiting for.

"Perfect," he says before Jakub can respond. "Looks like everything is starting to close up here. Probably time for us to head over to Rowan's, yeah? Do you want—"

"Okay, let's go." Jakub turns away from me and starts toward the exit, pushing Rafe along with him.

"We'll see you there!" Rafe calls back over his shoulder as Jakub all but shoves him outside.

"Uh, yeah, sounds good." But I'm not sure if he hears me. That all happened so fast, and I watch them through the windows as they walk to Rafe's truck, talking and gesturing animatedly once they get outside.

I could swear Rafe was about to ask if I want a lift to the party. Sure, Jakub will be at the party, but for a while it would be just me and Rafe.

But no, Jakub had to ruin it. "Cockblock," I mutter as I head out to my own car, digging through my bag for my keys and grumbling as my skates clobber my sore back again.

Maybe I can get Rafe alone at the party. I mean, he can't be glued to Jakub's side the entire time. Right?

It's useless. While Rafe hasn't been glued to Jakub, he's been so occupied by other people that I haven't been able to get within a foot of him.

I scrunch my nose at the crowd around him from across the room as I pour a hefty glug of vodka into a cup containing a much smaller amount of lemon-lime soda at the kitchen island. Having to watch this disaster unfold in real time, I need something stronger than wine. The ratio of vodka to soda has been leaning steadily in vodka's favor as the night has gone on, to the point that I can't even taste it anymore.

"Want to talk about it?" Jakub steps up to the other side of the island and sets out two cups.

"No." I don't know if he's offering to play therapist for my current bad mood, or if he's referring to the orgasm-shaped elephant between us, but either way, I'm not interested.

"I see." Jakub nods slowly, his focus completely on adding ice to both cups.

I sip my drink, watching Rafe laugh at something one of the girls around him just said.

He looks over to see what I'm staring at, then back at his cups. With a deep sigh, he says, "What do you want me to do? Set you up with him?"

My gaze snaps to his, and I narrow my eyes. There's no way he's seriously offering. Maybe he's saying it so he can somehow embarrass me in front of Rafe and ensure that Rafe never thinks of me that way. Maybe that's the reason he fooled around with me the other night. Not because he was half-asleep and didn't think about what he was doing, but to ruin my chances with his best friend.

To what end though? I'd think it's so he doesn't have to spend time with me, but he lives in my house. There's no getting out of seeing me, even if I'm not dating his best friend.

"Real funny," I tell him. "Don't say things you don't mean."

"Okay." Jakub grabs the handle of the nearest bottle and takes a swig straight from it before adding a bit to one of the cups. I notice that the other cup does not get any booze.

"What do you mean, 'okay'?" I drop my voice to just above a whisper. "Even if you did set me up with Rafe, that wouldn't even begin to cover all of the terrible shit you've pulled on me over the years."

Jakub looks up, surprised. "What terrible shit?"

"Did you think you were the only one up for that position at KLR? That job was mine until you went to lunch with Hank, and the next thing I knew, I was passed over for the boys' club."

"So...I got a job you wanted? That's the 'terrible shit I've pulled on you'?"

"You really want me to list every time you've deliberately ruined something for me since freshman year? I'm not sure the party is going to last that long."

"Okay." Jakub nods slowly, then takes another swig from the whiskey bottle. "Sure. Fine. I won't stand in the way between you and Rafe. Do you want me to move out immediately, or can I at least take enough time to search for an apartment?"

I couldn't be more surprised if he had just slapped me across the face. Did he really offer to move out?

I glance across the room to Rafe, who is now chatting with the boyfriend of one of my teammates. If I kick Jakub out now, he'll probably end back up on Rafe's couch. Which would make me look bad in front of Rafe. Which would be a real roadblock in my efforts to get him to fall for me.

Like it or not, I might have to learn to get along with Jakub if I stand any chance of ever dating Rafe. We don't have to be friends, but we need to at least not be completely at each other's throats.

"You can stay for now." I put the cap back on the soda and pick up my drink.

"Here. I was going to bring him this, but why don't you go give it to him instead?" Jakub holds out the cup with whiskey and soda.

I hesitate, wondering what the catch is, but I can't see one. He shakes the cup a little, urging me to take it.

"Fine." I swipe the cup out of Jakub's hand with a little more force than is probably necessary, sloshing a little bit over the side and onto my hand. I lick it off as I pick my way through the crowd.

I nearly trip on someone's shoe that's sticking out into a walking area, but I make it over to Rafe without spilling any more of his drink and squeeze in beside him. He startles a little, but smiles down at me when I hold out the drink.

"Oh, thank you." He accepts the cup and goes back to chatting with his friend.

I look around the room, noting all the other women eyeing Rafe. Well, too bad for them. I fought my way through the gauntlet to his side, and there's no way I'm giving the spot up so soon. Not without at least trying to join his conversation.

Too bad the conversation is boring as hell. I stay by his side, sipping my own drink as I listen to them discuss a very specific type of joint work. I've talked to Rafe about his furniture before, but it's never been this boring before. The guy he's talking to must also do woodworking, because they're deep in a hyper-detailed discussion of something so dull I can't follow the thread of conversation at all.

Occasionally Rafe looks over and smiles at me, but he doesn't make an effort to include me in the chat. He's not pushing me away though, so I stick it out. Eventually this woodworking talk will have to wear itself out and we can talk about literally anything else.

My attention begins to wander around the party again, and I do a double-take when I see my teammate Roxy standing very much in Jakub's personal space, with her shirt very much not covering her body anymore. I'm not surprised to see her lifting it to show him the mermaid she has inked below her left breast, because she's always quick to show off any amount of skin to good looking guys. It's like her own personal play book. Show a few stomach tattoos and then ask if they want to go somewhere a little more private to see her more personal ones up close. But Jakub doesn't look nearly as into it as most guys. In fact, he doesn't look into it at all. I watch as he looks around for an escape, too polite to just walk away but not actually engaging with her, however, she's got him backed into a literal corner.

If it was anyone else, I would go over there and save him. But I'm here with Rafe, and Jakub can handle himself. Besides, Roxy won't keep at it once she realizes he's truly not interested.

I try to keep my focus on what Rafe is saying, but my gaze keeps slipping back to Jakub and Roxy. Before I know it, my cup is empty, and I cannot keep listening to this boring conversation without more to drink. Maybe I'll even point out the group of cute guys in the living room and suggest Roxy go show them her mermaid.

I raise my cup to silently indicate to Rafe that I'm going for a refill. He barely acknowledges me with a short nod, not pausing his conversation as I slip away from his side.

Glancing back, I see that another girl I don't know is already taking up my spot beside Rafe. But she's not waiting for him to invite her into the conversation. Her hand is already on his arm and she's chatting away like she knows all there is to know about woodworking. I don't know, maybe she does. For her sake, I hope so, or she's going to be bored very soon.

I look to my left as I scoop more ice into my cup. Jakub's still being chatted up by Roxy. I could save him, but I'm not in the mood. In general, this party isn't fun anymore. I down my drink and immediately pour another, then go off in search of Daphne.

As usual, she's sitting in the corner watching everyone else have a good time instead of participating herself.

I plop down on the sofa next to her and rest my head on her shoulder, careful to hold my drink level so I don't spill.

"You okay?" She rests her head on top of mine and we look out at the party-goers together.

"Rafe is chatting up another girl." I sip more of my drink.

"Is he really? Or is he just talking to another girl?"

"Does it matter?" I look again to where Jakub is still in Roxy's clutches. She has a lot of tattoos, but could it really be taking this long? I can't believe she hasn't lost interest by now.

"I'm sorry." Daphne turns her head to kiss my hair before sipping her own drink. "What are you going to do about it?"

"I'm going to go home and be sad in my own bathtub. Maybe ice my hip and watch a baking TV show." I stand and throw back the last of my drink, wobbling a little on my feet.

"How many have you had?" Daphne's eyes cut to me before going back out to the crowd. Probably keeping an eye out for Rowan. "Do you think you should be driving?"

"Ha! No. No, I should not. Will you drive me? Otherwise, I can order a ride I guess." I'm not sure how many I've had, but it's enough that I am in no shape to get behind the wheel. I'll just have to come back tomorrow for my car.

"Well, Rowan is still here..."

"Because it's his house," I point out. I really hope she's not about to tell me no so that she can stay here and watch Rowan chat up all the women here except for her. She's spent enough parties doing that. "Besides, it's not like you're having a Helvetica good time."

I wait, knowing she hates when I make puns and always calls me out on them. Maybe it'll distract her from watching Rowan line up tonight's hookup long enough for me to drag her away.

She makes a face. "Now I'm definitely not driving you

home, but I'll sit here with you while you wait for your rideshare to arrive."

Sitting back down beside her, I rest my head in my hand for a moment. I'd really hoped Daphne would take me home so I don't have to make small talk with a random stranger tonight. I'm very much over this party and just want to be in my own space, alone.

"Everything okay?"

I look up to see Jakub hovering over me. Guess Roxy finally got the hint.

"Sera wants to go home, but she's not in a state to drive herself," Daphne says before I can come up with a good response to make him go away.

"I can take her," he replies immediately. When I glare at him, he chuckles and adds, "It'll be a Helvetica good time."

"I don't want to go home with you." I don't know what his ulterior motive is, but he must have one.

"Well, we live in the same place so I'm already going there," he reminds me. "And it's not like I'm going to try anything untoward. You've already made it clear that you have a crush on my best friend."

"Just let him take you home so you don't have to get a rideshare," says Daphne. She sounds like a beleaguered parent who has answered, "How much longer till we get there?" a dozen times in ten minutes.

"You're both annoying." I go back into the kitchen to toss my empty cup in a trash bin, and they trail behind me as though they're afraid I'm going to sneak out the back door and drive myself home. I turn around and face them. "Fine. Come on, let's go."

I don't stick around to say goodbye to anyone. My teammates won't be offended. Jakub follows me as I barrel out of the house and across the street to where his car is parked.

I pull on the handle, but it doesn't open. I try a few more times without success.

Finally, Jakub comes around to my side of the car and pushes the button on the key to unlock it. He crowds my space as he opens the door for me.

"I could have done it once it wasn't locked." I climb into the car and yank the door closed.

While he jogs around the front of the car, I look around and notice that it's actually clean in here. And now that I think about it, I haven't noticed any messes around the house since he's moved in. Unless he's keeping all of his clutter in his room, Jakub appears to be a surprisingly tidy man.

Hanging from the rearview mirror is a little figurine of a cat that looks a lot like Lucy. I reach up and turn it in my hands, inspecting it.

"I found an artist who, you send them pictures of your cat and they hand-mold clay to make an exact replica of them. Lucy was very impressed with how it turned out," says Jakub, sliding into the driver's seat.

"Are you sober enough to drive?" I remember watching him drink whiskey straight from the bottle not that long ago.

"I only had those two swallows you saw me take tonight," says Jakub, starting up the car. He pulls away from the curb and is turning off of Rowan's street before he speaks again. "I take it things didn't go well with Rafe."

"Only because that other guy was dominating the conversation." I lean my head back against the headrest and stare out the window. "If it had been just us, it would've been great."

"Whatever you say." His tone makes it clear he doesn't believe me, but he doesn't poke at me anymore and I promised myself I'd try to get along with him, so I let it go.

The rest of the ride is silent and as soon as he stops the

car in the driveway, I shove open the door and stumble up to the house. I'm just reaching the porch steps when Jakub's hand settles on the small of my back, steadying me as I use the railing for balance.

"I don't need help." I do feel less wobbly with both him and the railing, though. I should not have had as much to drink as I did. I need water.

"I know." But he keeps his hand there as he unlocks the front door with the other.

The lamp is on, once again.

"Honey, we're home!" he calls into the house, tossing his keys toward the base of the lamp.

Lucy makes cute little trilling noises as she trots down the stairs to greet us. Well, she's probably just greeting her dad, since until last night she barely acknowledged my existence, and I suspect I only had her attention last night because Jakub was out.

"Oh, my love, how was your evening?" Jakub scoops her up and buries his face in her soft fluff. She headbutts him, purring so loud I can hear it from six feet away. "Tell me all about it."

"More women fawning over you, lovely," I grumble under my breath as I climb the stairs, making sure to fully hold onto the railing as I go up.

"What was that?" he asks.

"Nothing." I reach the top of the stairs, relieved to be so close to falling into my comfy bed and putting an end to this stupid night.

"Drink some water," Jakub calls up after me.

I wave a hand in the direction of the downstairs, indicating I'd like him to kindly shut up, but I'm not sure he's even looking.

When I get to my room, there's a cat-sized impression on my once-perfectly spread forest green duvet, dusted with white fur. I guess I forgot to close my door earlier, so I make sure to do that now. With Jakub home, Lucy has no reason to want to be in my room, but just in case. Because if she comes in here, then Jakub has a reason to come in here, and I do not want that. Best to keep both Lucy and her dad out of my room.

Chapter Twelve

Ugh. I should not have had so much to drink at the party. It wasn't my intention to get hammered, but between Rafe inviting Jakub to the party and then watching Rafe entertain his adoring fan club all night, I was drowning my annoyance.

I grab my phone off the nightstand and text Daphne. *Did I embarrass myself last night?*

It must be pretty late in the morning, because she texts back almost immediately. *No, but it's probably a good thing you left when you did.*

Well, that sounds ominous, but I don't want to ask what happened. Most likely, she either means I was about to be a messy drunk, or Rafe kissed someone or something after I left. Neither of those things will make me feel better when I'm hungover and barely awake.

I decide to change the subject. *How did things go with Rowan?* She hadn't left the party to take me home, so maybe she was gearing up to actually go talk to him.

I left after he went upstairs with some redhead.

So much for that theory. Even from across the city, I can

feel how small she feels. I hate that this keeps happening to her.

Ugh, I'm sorry, Daph. Tell you what, I need to go get my car. Can you take me, and we can go do a fun girls' day on the way? If I can get Daphne out of the house, maybe I can distract her from feeling sad.

I have a virtual puzzle competition at 11 a.m., but I can take you later.

Thank you, you're the best. I'll have to think of something special to cheer her up. Good thing I've got some time. I'll be able to have caffeine first to get my mind going.

As soon as I open my bedroom door, I smell coffee. I wonder if it's too much to hope that Jakub will have made the coffee and then gone out, so I won't have to see him.

The tantalizing smell carries me down the stairs and into the kitchen. As soon as the door swings close behind me though, I know that luck isn't on my side today.

Yet again, Jakub is in my kitchen, drinking from my favorite mug and stirring something in a large mixing bowl. At least this time he's in his bathrobe instead of just boxers. His bare legs are sticking out from the bottom and I try not to notice that Daphne's suspicions were correct. He does have nice legs, not too hairy, and I've never paid attention to his feet before but they're also surprisingly not gross or weird. I don't know why I've always assumed he was some sort of hobbit-gremlin under his jeans and T-shirts, but as much as I wish I didn't have to see him at all today, it's at least nice to realize he's not, like, covered in scales or anything.

Grabbing my second favorite mug from the cupboard, I pour coffee into it. There's just barely enough for a cup.

"I'm making pancakes." Jakub sets the bowl next to the stove and reaches into a cupboard for a frying pan. "Do you want pancakes?"

The kitchen door swings a little and Lucy slinks in, curling herself forward around the bottom edge of the cupboards and making that cute chirping sound she does. She looks up with big eyes at her dad, glances at me, and then returns her gaze to Jakub. Okay, I guess we're only friends when he's not around then.

"The pancakes aren't for you, my love," says Jakub, ladling out the first round of batter.

Lucy's responding meow is clearly a grumble. I'm not a cat person and even I can tell.

"I guess I'll have some," I say. They're barely grilling but they smell so good. Exactly what I need to help with this hangover before it really settles over me. Remembering my decision to try to coexist more peacefully with him, I add, "Thanks."

He glances at me with a look of surprise, but quickly schools his features back to neutral and returns his attention back to the pan. "I'm planning to go to the store this morning for groceries," he says, flipping the cakes. "I could drop you off at your car on the way if you want."

I stare at his back and take a sip of coffee. First he's offering me pancakes, and now he's going to drive me to my car? Why is he being so nice?

"Okay," I say cautiously. I don't know what's going on with him, but I won't find out if I don't play along. Daphne and I can still hang out later even if I don't need her help to get my car.

Jakub plates up a stack of pancakes and sets them in front of me with silverware and syrup.

I doubt he's done anything to the pancakes, but just in case, I wait until he sits across from me at the table with his own plate and tucks in before I venture a taste of my own.

The first bite is so good, it's annoying. Is there anything this man isn't good at? The pancakes melt in my mouth and barely even need syrup because they're already so delicious. This is exactly what my stomach needs to mop up any remaining alcohol in my system after last night.

It's a little weird to sit here silently eating across from Jakub, but it's even weirder that we have an audience. Lucy has planted herself in the middle of the kitchen mat in front of the sink and is watching us with an intense focus.

Jakub finishes his stack of pancakes first, plowing through them while I'm savoring each bite.

"I cooked, you clean." He maneuvers around Lucy, who doesn't move from the spot she's claimed on the mat, and sets his dishes in the sink. "I'm going to jump in the shower and then we can leave."

And there's the catch I didn't see earlier. Who knew making pancakes resulted in this much mess on the counter and this many dishes? They never show this part in my favorite baking shows. Did he use extra utensils on purpose to spite me?

I pile the dishwasher-safe dishes into the dishwasher, careful not to disturb Lucy, but apparently I do anyway because she gives another complaining meow.

"Well, you need to sit somewhere else, then," I respond. "I need to clean up."

Great, now I'm talking to a cat. I rush through handwashing the pan and wiping down the counters, a challenge because I'm trying to give Lucy the room she seems to require. It would be so much easier if she would just move. She's probably trying to make my life harder on purpose. Like father, like daughter.

It's harder to make myself climb into Jakub's car without the balm of alcohol to give me a reason. I could wait for Daphne, but I've already agreed to let Jakub drive me, and who knows how long her competition will take. She's really fast at puzzling, but I don't know how the virtual competitions work, if she has to wait around for anything once she's done.

As soon as we're shut into the small space alone together, the fresh smell of his soap fills the air. And of course it smells good. Perfect-at-everything Jakub wouldn't have bad-smelling soap.

Something beeps, and an incoming message notification appears on the car's dashboard touchscreen. Jakub taps it, and the car announces, "Jenna says, 'I'm so glad you reached out to me. I'd love to see your talent in person. Let me know when you'd like to set something up.' Would you like to reply?"

"No," Jakub tells it, leaving me to wonder who Jenna is and what the message is about. It sure sounds like a hookup request, and it sounds like he reached out to her. When? After we fooled around? I shouldn't be upset that he's messaging another woman to hook up with so soon after our encounter in the basement, because I'd honestly rather forget that ever even happened, but it still stings to think that it left so little of an impression on him that he'd immediately be texting someone else to erase the memory.

It's not like I can call him out on it without acknowledging what we did though, and it's not like I really care that he's got someone else. But he didn't have to play the message for me to hear. He could have checked it after he drops me off at my own car.

We sit in complete silence for the rest of the drive to Rowan's neighborhood. Jakub pulls up right next to my tiny orange hatchback and waits for me to get out.

I mumble a thank you as I get out of the car, because I've decided to be the bigger person and try to get along with him. He doesn't reply, and I've barely even climbed into my driver seat before Jakub's driving away. He doesn't even toss me a wave.

Rude.

I'm wondering what my next move should be when my phone vibrates with an incoming text from Daphne.

Just finished my competition. Should I come pick you up to grab your car?

No need, I already got it. I'll tell her in person that Jakub not only brought me to get my car, but offered to do so unprompted. *Want to meet for coffee?*

I barely had a cup this morning and I don't want to go home and end up comparing my coffee-making skills to Jakub's superior ones. But I do very much need more caffeine.

I'll leave for D&D now, Daphne texts back.

Traffic is light until I get near the café. I forgot it was a weekend and would be packed. Oh, well. Too late now.

I keep an eye out for a table while I wait for my order. One has to open up at some point. There seems to be a new barista training today, making things run extra slowly.

Normally, I'd chat a little, but it's clear they're barely keeping up with the orders and don't need a distraction.

After a few minutes, I catch sight of a couple leaving so I scurry over to nab their empty seats.

When Daphne steps inside, her eyes go big with surprise at the long line and full tables.

I catch her attention and wave her over as she hovers near the end of the line.

"I already ordered for us," I say as she settles across from me.

"You bought me a drink twice in a row?" she teases. "What did I do to deserve this?"

"It's just because I love you."

"Liar."

"I had to wait for a table anyway so I figured I'd wait in line," I admit.

"And there it is," she says, sitting back in her chair, but stands up again almost immediately when my name is called. "You paid, I'll carry the drinks."

I watch as she Daphne carefully balances the coffees while she walks from the bar to our little table. I'm sure it's not easy with her long, flowy patchwork skirt trying to get twisted up between her legs. Plus, the cups are a little too full, no doubt why a little splashed over the side into the saucers. But there are beautiful little designs in the foam on top. Maybe that's why the barista is backed up, she's busy doing art when she should probably just hurry through the stack of waiting orders. I hope she doesn't get yelled at for it.

"How did your puzzle competition go?" I turn my coffee cup so the handle fits my fingers and I can cup the warmth for coziness.

"Really well," says Daphne before taking a cautious sip of her own coffee. "I submitted my time and video so hopefully they'll announce the winners this afternoon. But I feel good about it."

"That's great. And how was the rest of the party after I left?" I almost don't want to ask, but I have to know if Rafe was the reason she said it was good I left when I did.

"Fine." Daphne sighs. "Rowan spent most of the evening with Tegan, but she took off right after you and Jakub left, and he went upstairs almost immediately with that girl."

Daphne doesn't look sad when she says this, but she does look resigned. I want to reach over and cover her hand with mine to comfort her, but she would shake me off. She doesn't want pity. Or advice. I've told her dozens of times to either make a move or move on. She either doesn't want to, or she can't.

"So who took you to pick up your car?" She sits back, more relaxed now that she's changed the subject.

"Jakub." I sip my coffee and look out the window so I don't have to see her reaction.

"I'm guessing he offered, since you already had a ride lined up and wouldn't have needed to ask?"

I turn my head to look at her, but I can't read her expression. "He was going to the store anyway and said he could drop me off."

"Convenient," she deadpans, crossing her legs and sipping her drink.

"Some girl named Jenna texted him while we were driving to set up a time for him to 'show her his talents.'" I make air quotes with the hand that's not holding my drink.

"Huh, that's weird. Are you sure that's what she meant?"

"She didn't come out and say, 'let's set up a sex date,' but she did say they should set up a time to get together." I set my cup down in the saucer with a clink. "Wait, why is that weird? Do you think it was about something else?" I don't know what it could be, or why she would know about it, but I suppose it's possible it wasn't a booty call text.

"Oh, no reason." Daphne responds too quickly, and even waves a hand to dismiss my question. "By the way, I heard a weather report on my way here and they said there's another storm forecasted for tonight."

"How bad?" I'm already pulling out my phone to check the radar.

"High winds and high probability of thunderstorms."

Daphne sips her coffee as she sits back serenely in her chair, still looking like she's got a secret.

"Looks like it shouldn't start until late, so at least I don't have to spend the entire day in the basement." I move the sliding bar at the bottom of the map to move the time projection forward to follow the storm.

"But you'll probably want to sleep down there, right?" I don't like the smile she's got on her face, and when she speaks again. "Think Jakub will join you again?"

"I hope not." We're already ignoring what happened between us, and I have no choice about sleeping downstairs, but he does. Surely he wouldn't put us in a position to have to share a bed again.

Chapter Thirteen

I've been keeping an eye on the radar all day in case things change. I've been hoping the storm will dissipate and I can sleep in my own bed, but nope.

I grab my pillow and close my bedroom door so Lucy won't sleep in my bed. She's been getting very comfy in my room when I've left it open.

Jakub's voice stops me in my tracks just before I hit the stairs.

"Bad weather again?" He sticks his head out of his bedroom door.

"Yeah," I reply hesitantly.

He ducks back into his room. "Lucy, come here, love."

I should leave. I should go to the basement and hope he doesn't follow me. But for some reason, I stay in the hall, waiting.

"I'm not sure where she is." Jakub appears in the doorway with his own pillow.

Daphne was right.

"You don't have to come." There's no reason for it. He's not afraid of storms, I assume, like I am.

He looks at me like I've just suggested he lick an outlet. "Safety first."

"I really think you'll be fine."

He cocks his head to the side. "But you won't be?"

"It's complicated," I tell him, turning to descend the stairs.

He follows me. "Complicated how?"

"Just...complicated."

He's right on my heels as we make our way to the basement door. "Try me."

I let out a frustrated groan and yank the door open. "Okay, fine, it's not that complicated. I just get freaked out during storms, okay?

I stomp down the stairs, irritated that he got me to admit my stupid phobia out loud.

"Any particular reason?" He sounds genuinely curious, not like he's making fun of me, and when I glance back at him, he isn't smirking or anything.

Sighing, I admit that there isn't. "I grew up in the Midwest. Tornadoes are a real threat there. At some point as a kid I guess I decided that all storms were as scary as tornadoes, and even though I know it's stupid, I've never been able to shake it."

I tug the cushions off the sofa and Jakub pulls the mattress out.

"It's not stupid," he tells me. "If you're scared, you're scared. It doesn't have to make sense." He balances his pillow on the back of the sofa next to mine and I think for a moment that he might be about to help me make the bed.

"I'm going to find Lucy. I don't want her upstairs by herself if the storm gets bad." Jakub disappears back up the stairs.

If I had a lock on the basement door, I'd consider shutting him out. Instead, I stare at the way his black pillow is partially settled on top of my own. It looks way too intimate, our pillows touching like that. I shouldn't even know what his pillow looks like.

With just two fingers I push his pillow to the cement floor and drop a heavy blue blanket on it. It didn't work last time, but maybe this time it will. At minimum, it'll signal to him that nothing is going to happen between us tonight. No matter how scary the storm is about to be, I am not letting myself get caught up in another mess like that.

I'm just tucking in the corners of the sheet when I hear Jakub coming down the stairs, whispering sweet nothings to Lucy. How beautiful she is, how he's so glad to have her in his life, how he'd be devastated if anything ever happened to her. Basically everything I've ever dreamed of Rafe saying to me.

Climbing into bed and adjusting my silky sleep shorts so they don't bunch up around my hips, I try to ignore Jakub and the way my stomach is flipping. It's probably just anxiety about the oncoming storm and knowing I'm not going to sleep well on this uncomfortable mattress with Jakub in the same room.

"We've been over this," says Jakub, setting Lucy down on the bed and picking up his pillow. "The floor is cold and I'm not sleeping on it."

He sets the pillow and blanket on the bed next to me, careful not to disturb Lucy, who is testing out where my legs are beneath the blankets. I hold my breath as he slides into bed next to me, spreading his blanket over himself on top of the comforter.

At least he keeps to his side of the bed. And he's not naked.

"We really should put up a TV down here," he says, looking around at the bare walls. "Make the place more comfortable."

"If it's comfortable, people might feel welcome down here." I give him a significant look. "I kind of like Rafe's home gym idea. I don't need another place for people to feel like they can get comfortable."

With that, I roll over away from him, careful not to disturb Lucy in the process. Just because he's here doesn't mean I have to give him my attention. So I focus on trying to sleep, even though I can see the glow of his phone and hear him breathing behind me, occasionally whispering loving words to Lucy. I hate that I find it so endearing.

Boom!

I jump, adrenaline flooding my veins, but at least I'm no longer waiting for the other shoe to drop. The storm is starting.

"Why don't you move over here?" Jakub asks softly, and my mind goes blank, unable to believe his audacity.

"There you go."

Oh. He was talking to Lucy. I relax a little.

My moment of relative calm doesn't last though, because he scoots his body right behind mine and rubs his hand soothingly up and down my upper arm. If there wasn't a storm beginning to rage outside, I'd pull away from Jakub's touch, but as much as I hate to admit it, it's comforting to not be alone. Another thunderclap booms, and my body shakes of its own accord. If I had the power, I'd never choose to be so afraid of storms. I've tried all the tricks, yet my brain tells me to panic and my body follows the order. I hate that Jakub is seeing me being so weak.

But he doesn't say anything mocking or mean. He just keeps rubbing my arm.

The next flash of lightning is almost immediately followed by the biggest boom yet. The storm is almost right upon us.

I grab Jakub's hand and pull it to my chest, wrapping his

arm around myself like a protective ward. Squeezing my eyes closed, I remind myself that this is as far as this goes, and it's only for the storm. After tonight, just like before, we're never going to talk about this again.

His fingers feel solid and thick when he laces them through mine, and I focus on just breathing through the storm. Jakub scooches closer, pressing his chest fully against my back to compensate for the way I'm holding his arm as if it is the only thing keeping me safe.

My heart is pounding in time with the rain pounding against the small basement windows. I pull up one of the techniques Daphne told me about that's supposed to help calm me down. I categorize and take note of everything I can feel or know to be happening in the room.

Jakub's hands. His hands are bigger than mine. They're coarser than I thought they would be, given that I've never known him to do anything that would produce callouses, but they're still soft.

Jakub's arm, pressing against mine as I hold him closer.

His chest is solid, molded to my back as he holds me.

His thighs are curled up beneath my own, so I'm practically sitting on his lap even though we're laying on our sides.

I realize that every single thing I've noted so far has to do with Jakub, so I scan about for something that isn't related to him. The bed. The awful mattress that I can almost feel every spring through. So many springs poking into me.

Lucy purring, somewhere in the darkness.

And something poking into my ass.

My mind skitters off course, jumping back to the last time we were in this exact situation. The way Jakub got me off. The fact that we never talked about it. How much it helped to distract me from the storm.

I had sworn nothing like that would happen again, but as I lie here, suddenly unable to think about anything except the way Jakub's cock is pressing against me and how wet I'm getting just remembering last time, I wonder if it would really be so bad to distract myself like that again. I mean, I had a good time, and I assume he did too or he wouldn't be back down here, spooning me with a hard-on. Like before, I subtly shift my hips a little, wondering if he'll take the bait.

He doesn't move, but I can feel him growing harder beneath my ass. After a moment, he rests his forehead on my shoulder, and I can hear him breathing like he's trying to steady himself.

I focus on waiting for Jakub to do something, barely noticing the next flash of light. The next big boom of thunder draws my attention for a moment, but I keep my eyes closed and force myself to set the fear crawling up my spine aside. If I'm thinking about Jakub, I can't think about the storm.

Finally, his thumb shifts slightly, dragging across the front of my shirt, right over the top of one breast.

There's another flash, so bright I can see it through my closed eyelids. One finger at a time, I release Jakub's hand. It's the closest I can come to vocalizing that I'm interested in letting him distract me. But only for tonight. Only for this storm.

Holding my breath, I wait for him to do something. Anything.

He releases his own breath against my shoulder as his thumb again drags against my shirt. If he moves his hand down just another inch, he'll be palming my breast. And I'm biting my lip, hoping it will happen.

Jakub's hand inches down at a snail's pace. I'm sure the whole time that he's going to pull back, roll away, and leave me here embarrassed. But he doesn't. He gently cups my breast, testing the weight of it, and I nearly sigh in relief that he's finally touching me.

The only thing that stops me is the fact that I don't want to do anything that will acknowledge that this is happening, that I'm enjoying the way he's touching me.

If Rafe were the one lying behind me on this bed, I'd already have rolled over and lifted my leg over his hip to give him easy access. But it's not Rafe, it's Jakub. If I don't say anything, don't move, don't breathe, then later on it'll be easier to pretend it never happened.

Jakub begins to knead my breast with his palm, molding my flesh like I'm clay and he's going to create art with my body.

Just as I'm settling into the rhythm of his movements though, he changes it up and focuses solely on my nipple, pebbled beneath my thin T-shirt. The fact that I'm so wet from his ministrations speaks volumes, which I'll never voice aloud, about how talented this man's fingers are. If my body fully understood how much my brain dislikes Jakub, it would not be reacting this way.

My ass shifts against Jakub's hard cock again as I move my bottom leg, bringing my knee up, and stretch the top one toward the foot of the bed to give Jakub more access to the spot where need is coiling between my legs. If he's interested in taking it, that is. To distract me from the storm raging outside. Because that's all this is, a distraction. When the storm passes and the sun comes up, we're never going to talk about this again.

Jakub's free arm slides beneath my pillow and I lift my head a little to let him wrap his hand around my body and caress my other breast.

When he moves his top hand away a moment later, I nearly bite through my lip to keep myself from whimpering in displeasure.

Slowly, Jakub inches his hand down my side, scrunching my shirt up into his fist. With each inch of my stomach exposed, he pauses, as if waiting for me to stop him. Stopping him is the furthest thing from my mind though.

My breathing is irregular with need, and I'm sure he can tell. My heart is pounding, and even with the blankets only covering our lower halves, it's suddenly so warm in this bed that I contemplate throwing them off entirely. But if I were to do that, it would break the spell, forcing us to acknowledge what's happening, and I'm not ready to do that.

Soon, my shirt is bunched up over my breasts, giving Jakub full access to my bare skin. His fingertips explore every inch of my chest. A shiver runs through me as the cool air hits my nipples. It's such a contrast to the heat of Jakub's body pressed against my back.

With the wind rattling the basement windows as a soundtrack, his fingers blaze a trail down my bare stomach and over my navel, brushing against the waistband of my sleep shorts. He pauses, probably expecting me to stop him, but I have no intention of doing that.

I roll my hips against his and that seems to be enough for him. Slowly, his fingers slip underneath my waistband.

Jakub's breath shudders as he realizes that I'm not wearing any underwear. Only sleep shorts.

He shows more restraint than I feel though, touching me everywhere but where I need him to.

Even fooling around, it's like he's purposely trying to frustrate me. If I weren't determined to stay silent, I'd tell him exactly how frustrated he's making me.

He must read my mind, because he moves his leg between mine so his cock is pressed even more against my ass. I hate how much I love the feel of his hands on me, although I wish he'd put his fingers where I really need them.

When I can't take his teasing anymore, I wrap a hand around his forearm and guide his hand between my thighs.

Jakub huffs a laugh against my shoulder, and it occurs to me that I may have just handed him the game.

But as soon as Jakub traces a single finger through my slit and realizes how wet I am, his chuckle switches to a groan and he nestles his face into the crook of my neck. Maybe I haven't lost after all. And when he dips his fingertips into my juices to drag them up and circle my clit, I lose track of who's winning because it feels so good.

My grip on Jakub's forearm tightens as he circles my clit tightly and then presses against it with the heel of his hand as he slides a single digit into my dripping pussy.

I roll my hips, trying to take his finger even deeper, and I can feel him thrusting his hard cock against my ass as I ride his hand.

It's not enough though. I'm about to break my no-talking rule and ask him to add a second finger, maybe even a third, but again he reads my mind, slipping a second finger inside me, and I moan as he curls them against my g-spot just as his palm drags over my clit. Thunder booms outside, and I still want more, want to be stretched, want to be filled so completely that I don't have room to think about anything but how good he's making me feel.

Jakub's cock grinds harder against my ass, and his breath is getting rougher and more ragged.

Turning my head into my pillow, I bite the pillowcase to keep from crying out. I'm so close. Just a little...bit...more...

My hips buck against Jakub's hand and I come so hard it blocks out everything around me.

His own thrusts become more erratic until he groans and collapses on top of me. His weight presses me into the mattress as we both slowly come down from the orgasmic haze.

Like last time, he rolls away from me after a moment.

Unlike last time, I sort of wish he hadn't.

I must have fallen asleep, because the sudden boom of thunder is much closer than it had been before. It had faded off into the distance shortly after Jakub rolled away from me, but nature must have decided on another round just in case the last one wasn't enough torture.

The thunder must have awoken Jakub too, and he doesn't pause before his hands are on me. Everywhere. My shirt is still rucked up right under my arms, and one of his hands is already seeking out my nipples, and the other is sliding between my folds.

"I have a condom." Jakub nips at the back of my neck with his teeth.

I don't move, and except for his fingers rubbing slow circles over my clit, neither does he.

When did he go get a condom? Did he bring it down here to begin with or did he sneak off at some point while I was asleep?

Do I want to use it?

The storm rages outside, making me shiver. Jakub's breath ruffles my hair as he waits for me to answer his unspoken question.

Surprising as it is, I've loved having Jakub's hands on me. He's made me feel good, not just distracted. I'd never admit it to him, but he's probably the best fuck I've ever had, and we haven't even fully fucked yet.

Wait. Yet? Did I really just think that I haven't fucked him *yet*? Do I actually want to fuck Jakub?

I think I might.

This realization is startling, and I wonder if he'll be surprised if I agree. "Okay," I whisper.

His hand pauses briefly, and I mentally will him to start moving it again.

"Yes?" he asks, but he doesn't sound surprised as much as he seems to be confirming, giving me an opportunity to change my mind.

I'm not going to change my mind. The instant I said 'okay,' I knew it was what I want. "Yes."

I assume he'll roll over, retrieve the condom from wherever he's stashed it, and immediately get to work, but he doesn't. Instead, he continues touching me. Rolling my nipples between his deft fingers and slowly stroking between my folds. Warming me up, although my body is responding so quickly that he really doesn't need to. He's clearly already ready, if the way his cock is again pressing against my ass is any indication.

When I'm wound tight as a spring from the way the pads of his fingers have been gliding over my clit and have soaked through my sleeping shorts, I take things into my own hands and shimmy them over my hips and down my legs. I kick them out from beneath the blankets to land on the floor.

Only then does Jakub pull away, and for a moment, I consider that this could be a big joke that he's playing on me. But then I hear the crinkle of a condom packet in the darkness, and he's back, his chest pressed against my back, our bare legs tangling together.

I'm gasping with need, already bringing up one knee to give him more access.

He strokes the head of his cock through my folds, then

rolls me over onto my stomach before notching himself at my entrance.

Jakub pauses as he always does, giving me an opportunity to back out, but I've made my choice. I press my hips back so the tip of his cock slips into my pussy. He lets out a breath against my neck and eases forward slowly to fully sheath himself inside my wet heat.

The stretch is glorious, and I'm glad he didn't just shove himself inside. He's not monstrously large, but it's been a while and he's still a good size. It's so weird to think that it's Jakub of all people who's buried to the hilt inside me, and even weirder to realize that he fills me more perfectly than any other man I've been with.

I don't want to think, though. I only want to feel. Now that he's in, he's waiting again, and I'm desperate for him to move already.

It's difficult with his weight pinning me to the bed, but I roll my hips a little bit, sliding his cock partway out and then back in. I only manage to get two hip rolls in before Jakub nudges my legs apart with his knees and sinks his cock even deeper into my slick pussy, hitting a spot so good that a moan of pleasure escapes me before I can stop it. He takes the sound as the encouragement that I suppose it is, pulling out and sliding forward again as I raise my ass to meet his hips.

I won't let him have full control, no matter how good it would feel to let him hold me down and have his way with me. I continue to push my hips back against him so that we match each other thrust for thrust, and it's more aggressive than any first time I've ever had with a man. But it feels so good to use each other like this. Overwhelming and slightly punishing, like we're creating our own storm here inside the basement, under these blankets, crashing into each other as the thunder crashes outside.

Or maybe we're racing. As his movements become faster and more intense, I'm growing desperate to reach the orgasm he's building to a crescendo inside me.

When Jakub reaches around and slides his hand between me and the mattress to press two fingers against my clit, I explode. I cry out, my eyes rolling back into my head and my limbs going tingly as the inferno courses through my veins.

Just as my climax begins to ebb, Jakub's fingers slide apart so they're on either side of my clit, applying a less direct pressure to the sensitive area as he slams into me three more times. On the third thrust, a second orgasm racks my body, and he lets out a groan as he also comes apart. With a final thrust, he collapses on top of me, his own breathing heavy and his cock twitching inside me as my walls pulse around it.

I stare into the darkness, my heart hammering against my ribs. I can't believe that just happened. And I can't believe that I enjoyed it.

Chapter Fourteen

When I wake in the dim light of morning, I glance over my shoulder to see that Jakub is still asleep, pressed up against my back with one arm thrown over my waist.

I never would have pegged Jakub as a snuggler.

Slowly I slide out from beneath his weight. It's only once I'm out from beneath the covers that I remember I'm not wearing shorts. I search the floor and find them a good few feet from the bed, sliding them on just in case Jakub wakes up. He might have been inside me in the dark, but I'm not ready for him to see me in the daylight yet. I find my phone and turn off the alarm that's set to go off in a few minutes so it doesn't wake up Jakub. I don't want to have to face him yet.

Before I walk away, I look back one more time. Jakub is curled on his side, his expression slightly perturbed even in sleep, and his hand is spread out in the spot I've just vacated. Adorably though, Lucy is curled up on top of the blanket behind the crook of his knees, her paw covering her nose. It's so cute I almost *aww* out loud.

Instead, I tear my eyes away and creep toward the stairs. I need a shower, coffee, and food. In that order.

I tiptoe up to the kitchen, careful not to put my weight on the squeaky third step. I start to close the door behind me, then hesitate. I should leave it open so Lucy will be able to get out, but that will also allow the smell of coffee to drift down to Jakub, which might wake him up.

I settle on resting the door against the frame. Now Lucy can escape if she wants, but maybe the coffee smell won't drift downstairs as much. I start up the coffee pot and head upstairs for a much-needed shower. My thighs are sticky from the three—three!—orgasms Jakub gave me last night, and I want to scrub away all traces of our encounter so I can pretend it didn't happen. Just like before.

By the time I'm pouring coffee into my thermos decorated with the hex code for matcha green to perfectly match not only the thermos, but my derby uniform and my hair, I'm casting furtive glances at the basement door and listening intently for the sound of footsteps on the stairs. The door was ajar when I came down, so I guess Lucy came upstairs at some point. Which means that now Jakub can smell the coffee that was brewing while I showered.

I only take a full deep breath once I get outside and into my car without running into Jakub. I relax more and more as I drive to work, knowing that I have at least eight hours ahead of me where I won't have to worry about seeing him.

Every sip I take from my travel mug makes me grimace though. I can't believe I used to think this was good coffee. I hate that Jakub manages to make the same coffee so much better. Maybe one of these mornings I'll be able to see how he does it. It's not like he could be brewing it much differently than me.

No, I need to stop thinking about him. I have other frustrations to deal with today. Namely, my most annoying client, Arty. He's never going to be happy with the assets no matter how many tweaks I send over.

I've barely been at work for fifteen minutes when my phone beeps with a text and my heart rate jumps.

But it's only Daphne. *How was the storm?* Followed by a damn winky-face emoji.

I'm so glad it's not Jakub. Although, I realize with a start, it couldn't be because he still doesn't have my number. He's been inside me, but he can't call or text me. Something about that feels a little bit wrong. Maybe Rowan or Tegan would be fine with a hookup not being able to contact them again, but I've never been that kind of girl.

Not that I want Jakub to have my number. The whole situation is just strange.

It happened again, I text back. Daphne is my best friend, I can't keep this from her. I need someone to help me sort out my tangled thoughts about what keeps happening between me and Jakub in the basement. And it's not like I can talk to him about it.

Besides, it's not like Daphne doesn't already suspect we'd hooked up again.

What happened?

Don't play dumb. You know. Now that we're talking about it, flashes from last night are playing out in my mind like a poorly-lit porno. I can't believe Jakub went upstairs in the night to get a condom. And I also can't believe that I'm glad he did.

Holy shit. Then a bunch of laughing emojis. *I knew it. You 'accidentally' slept with your roommate again, didn't you?*

Shut up, I reply. Then, *...Twice.* My traitorous brain calls up the memory of being pressed into the mattress with him thrusting between my thighs, and my pussy responds immediately, clenching and dampening. *It wasn't my fault though. It was the storm.*

Suuure, she says. *I told you he was cute. I knew eventually you'd see reason.*

He's not bad looking, I grudgingly admit. *But it's not happening again. It shouldn't have happened to begin with. I like Rafe.*

If you say so. Daphne adds another little winky emoji.

I can't blame her for giving me grief. Goodness knows I'd be teasing her if our roles were reversed.

"Sera!" I look up to see my boss crossing the room to my desk. The whole office is unapologetically leaning in to listen as he says, "Arty called and complained that the assets for his website are trash."

"He keeps changing his mind about what he wants!" It's not fair for Bartholomew to be mad at me when it's the clients who keep moving the goalposts.

"That's not the problem," says my boss. "The problem is that you're not delivering quality work, so he isn't happy with what you send him."

I close my eyes to keep from exploding. *I need this job,* I repeat over and over in my head. "Okay," I say, my voice small and resigned. "I'll call him and see what he'd like me to change."

My entire body feels stiff. Taking a day off between a game and a full-on practice is supposed to be good for my body, but right now it doesn't feel that way. Not to mention, I took out my frustration at work and confusion at what's happening between me and Jakub on the track. It was effective; Rowan complimented my playing tonight. But now I feel like I'm dying.

I pull my car into the driveway and stare up at the front windows. They're bright behind the curtains, definitely more light than the foyer lamp alone would provide. My eyes slide to Jakub's car parked in front of mine in the driveway, and then back to the lights. He's definitely home, and hanging out downstairs. There will be no way for me to avoid him.

I don't want to go inside, but that's where my hot bath lives. The hot bath that I need to relax my sore muscles.

I let out a resigned sigh. I suppose I have to face him sometime.

Opening the front door, I peek through to the living room, but Jakub's nowhere in sight, and neither is Lucy. Maybe they're in his room and I can avoid him after all.

I'm about to head for the kitchen to get a glass of wine for the bath when I hear his voice coming from, of course, the kitchen.

Well, that settles that, then. I can take my bath without my glass of wine. I set my foot on the bottom step and am ready to begin the climb when I hear him say "Rafe", and my feet seem to carry me of their own accord into the kitchen.

Jakub is standing at the counter with an array of snacks spread out before him. Lucy sits on a pulled-out chair at the little bistro table.

They both glance up at me when I enter, and Jakub says into the phone, "Why don't we watch the game here instead?"

I move to the fridge and pull out the first thing I see, a glacial blue sports drink full of electrolytes, trying to look like that was the whole reason I came to the kitchen to begin with.

"See you soon." Jakub sighs as he hangs up the phone. He doesn't look at me as he puts together a plate of snacks, but he says, "Rafe is coming over. I'll make up an excuse to give the two of you some alone time."

Jakub's shoulders are stiff as he adds a handful of pistachios to his plate. My stomach twists. I fucked this man not twenty-four hours ago, yet here he is setting up an opportunity for me to spend time alone with his best friend.

I mean, I'm glad he's not making a big deal about what happened between us, but maybe I should say something? The look Lucy is giving me from the chair is pure judgement. I guess she doesn't approve of me fucking her dad and then letting him wingman for me.

I know, Lucy. It feels kind of gross to me too.

"Okay," I say slowly because I can't say nothing, but I can't bring myself to mention last night.

Uncomfortable, I don't look at him as I move to the cabinet where the plates live. I reach up to grab my own small plate to make a post-workout snack, since I'm in here anyway.

"What the fuck is that?" Jakub grabs the edge of my sweater and starts lifting it, exposing my stomach. I'm surprised by how upset he sounds.

"What are you doing?" I try unsuccessfully to bat his hands away. I'm not like Roxy, wanting to show off all my tattoos. I got them for me.

"There's a huge bruise on your side." He tugs my sweater up even more, fingers hovering over the purple splotch on my waist.

"Of course there is. The bout was only two days ago." I yank my sweater back down and take a step back, feeling self-conscious about him seeing any parts of my body that are normally covered, and then feeling silly about it. He's been inside me, for fuck's sake, I should not be weirded out by him seeing my midriff. But that was in the dark, and I didn't have to see his face as he looked at me. The concern in his eyes and the reminder of how good his hands felt on me are both things I'd rather not have to think about right now.

After an uncomfortable beat, he turns back to the counter and continues fixing his food.

"Does it hurt?" He glances over his shoulder at me as I begin to put together my own snacks.

"It's sore, but mostly from practice. Taking hits in the same spot was rough. But that's part of derby." I shrug. It's a full contact sport, bruises are par for the course.

He begins to gather up the food that we're both finished with. "Do you want to watch something while we wait for your crush to come over?"

The emphasis he puts on 'your crush,' like the words taste bad, make me look up, but I can't see his face.

"Sure."

It's hard to even contemplate being around Rafe right now. I'm still trying to figure out how to act around Jakub after last night.

I carry my plate into the living room and sit down on the sofa. Jakub follows, holding the swinging door open for Lucy as if she's walking a runway through the house.

He takes a step toward the sofa, but seems to think better of it and moves to sit in the chair where Rafe was last time instead. I'm sure he's just leaving the spot closest to me open for when Rafe gets here, and I should be glad he's keeping some distance between us, but I'm also a little... disappointed? No, that pang I felt cannot possibly be disappointment that Jakub doesn't want to sit with me. It's got to just be nerves, and excitement about Rafe coming over.

"Is there anything in particular you want to watch?" Jakub grabs the remote off the coffee table and starts flipping through channels as Lucy jumps up to sit next to me on the sofa. He looks over as she curls herself up against my leg, rubbing her cheek against my dress pants, and I swear he's giving us a look of longing. Probably wishing there was room for her on his chair so she could cuddle up to him instead.

"No." I can't even think of the names of any of the shows I like right now, too busy trying to analyze the situation that's currently happening between me and Jakub. It's one thing for me to think what happened between us doesn't matter, but I don't like that he's acting the same way. And I don't like that I don't like it. It's stupid to be hurt by someone wanting to pretend something didn't happen when that's exactly what I want too.

Jakub flips through the channel until he lands on a show about birds. Lucy immediately sits up, completely focused on the screen as she makes her little chattering noises. It's very cute, and makes me smile, a welcome distraction from the thoughts spinning through my head.

"You're such a good huntress," Jakub tells her, breaking open a pistachio. "You could definitely take down a bower bird."

Lucy, her eyes focused on the screen, chitters back as if in agreement. *I'm super fierce,* she seems to be saying. *I could easily take down this bower bird if only it wasn't on TV.*

We watch in silence, both of us more entertained by Lucy than by the show, and I make my way through my plate of snacks without tasting anything. I'm stress-eating, bothered by the fact that Jakub isn't looking at me or sitting by me and anxious that Rafe isn't here yet.

When my plate is empty and Rafe still isn't here, I can't take the tension any longer. I bring my plate into the kitchen, taking my time rinsing it and putting it in the dishwasher. When I return to the living room, I hover by the sofa again. I just can't sit here anymore in this awkwardness. Should I say something? Or just leave?

Jakub glances at me and then quickly back to his plate. Is it possible that he is also uncomfortable? The thought makes me feel a little better about my own discomfort, and I decide to extend an olive branch in the form of telling him that I'm going to take a quick shower. He nods, but doesn't look up or say anything.

Okay, then. At least I tried.

My bedroom door is partially open. I must have forgotten to close it this morning.

Based on the little indentation in the middle of my bed, Lucy at least was definitely in here at some point today for a nap. I can't be mad at her. She's too cute, and it's my own fault for leaving the door open.

I really want to soak in a hot bath, but I instead take the fastest shower I've ever taken as I debate what to wear when I get out. I could dress in my comfy pajamas and I'm so sore I'm tempted, but I don't want to look frumpy in front of Rafe. So I pull on my cutest jeans and a simple dark teal T-shirt with a slight V-neck. Rafe is so tall, it'll give him a good view of my boobs even while we're sitting on the sofa.

The front door opens and closes, and Rafe's voice floats up the stairs. I swipe on some light makeup, just enough that I don't look as exhausted as I am.

I make sure to time my entry into the living room so as not to be suspicious, and to give Rafe enough time to get settled so when I come in, he can adjust his focus completely to me.

"Thanks, man," I can hear Rafe say softly as I descend the stairs. "I really appreciate it."

I stop short coming around the newel post because Rafe is supposed to be sitting on the sofa so I can sit next to him, but he's in the chair. Leaving me sitting next to Jakub on the sofa.

"Hey," Jakub says when he sees me. He doesn't look thrilled, and shakes his head almost imperceptibly, his gaze flicking from me to Rafe and back again. I guess, somehow, his plan to leave the sofa for me and Rafe got thwarted.

"Hey, Sera," says Rafe, turning my way with a big smile on his face. "How are you feeling after that win this weekend? Motivated to keep it going?"

"Something like that." I chuckle as I slide between Jakub and the coffee table to sit back on the sofa. "We're going to give it our best, at any rate."

"She's covered in bruises," says Jakub. "You should go get some ice for that one on your side."

"I'm fine." I roll my eyes as I lean forward to grab the sports drink I left on the coffee table when I went upstairs. The high-rise of my jeans presses against my bruise, and I wince.

"That's because you're a badass athlete," agrees Rafe.

"Liar," Jakub whispers to me as he takes a sip of his own sports drink, a strawberry-kiwi one.

Which, once again, is one of mine. I'm not going to call him out on it right now, but he will be replenishing my supply the next time he goes to the store.

I'm not going to openly flirt with Rafe in front of Jakub, that would just be weird, so I choose a safe, neutral topic. "Where did Lucy go?"

"Her food dish went off in the kitchen," answers Jakub. His phone buzzes in his pocket, and when he pulls it out the screen is lit up with the word 'Jenna'—the same name as the girl who texted him that day in the car. "I have to take this."

I watch Jakub disappear up the stairs, noting that he doesn't answer the call until he's out of sight and keeps his voice too low for me to hear what he's saying.

"Rowan looks like he's put together a good team for this season," says Rafe, oblivious to the way I'm straining to hear Jakub's conversation.

"Yeah, everyone has been amazing to practice and compete with," I reply, but I'm still watching the stairs. "I'm really glad Daphne convinced me to try out." Has Jakub been talking to Jenna regularly, or is she reaching out to him because he hasn't gotten back to her about getting together? "Are you prepping for your upcoming lumberjack competition?"

"Yeah," Rafe chuckles a little.

I should be appreciating his laugh, the way it makes his wide shoulders bounce a little, but all I can think about is how Jakub fucked me last night in the basement and now he's upstairs making plans to hook up another woman.

"I've been chopping a lot of wood lately, making sure my axe is well-balanced," Rafe continues.

"And how are the orders for Adirondack chairs coming?" Rafe makes the most comfy-looking front porch chairs, and for a while it seemed like they were generating a lot of interest from people.

"I've actually switched it up and am focusing on dining room sets now. I like the clean lines of the Adirondacks, but the ornate scrollwork of dining sets has been amazing to get into lately." Rafe's face gets more animated as he discusses his work. "I may even figure out how to do some custom inlays at some point."

I finally pull my gaze away from the stairs.

"That's a big change." I hadn't realized Rafe could be so fickle about his woodworking. Doesn't he realize that picking a subset of furniture and honing in on that niche market is probably a better business model?

"You know how it is. The heart wants what the heart

wants." Rafe shoots me a wink and looks toward the stairs. "I wonder what's taking Jakub so long."

"Is there anything else new with you?" *Like maybe you went to a new restaurant and think we should check it out together? Or you know all the dirt on this Jenna person?*

"I got a new axe," says Rafe after thinking about it for a moment. "Well, not new-new, but new to me. A really good one that will last forever. It'll be much better for competitions than the one I've been using."

"Oh?" Really? A new axe? That's all he's got?

Apparently that's enough, because he starts going into great detail about it. He mentions brand and weight and balance and all sorts of things I really don't care about. Would it kill him to flirt a little? I try to think of something else to change the subject to, because I don't even know how to begin flirting when he won't shut up about the stupid axe, but all I can think of is to ask if he knows anything about Jenna. Which doesn't feel like a good topic to get him feeling flirty.

I find myself wishing, of all things, that Jakub would come back down. He could help steer the conversation back to something more interesting. But it seems he's so riveted by Jenna's conversational skills that he's completely forgotten that he invited his best friend over to hang out.

Or maybe he got bad news and he's upset? Maybe I should excuse myself and go check on him.

I'm about to do just that when Jakub reappears at the bottom of the stairs. "Sorry about that," he says, returning to his seat on the sofa.

"Everything okay?" Rafe asks. He also seems to have relaxed some now that Jakub is back down here with us.

"Oh, yeah." Jakub settles his arm along the back of the sofa and pats his lap for Lucy to jump up and join him. "We were just discussing the details for this weekend."

I stiffen at Jakub's words. He was confirming details for a date with Jenna this weekend? I startle a little when Lucy jumps up into my lap and then daintily walks across me to stretch out in the small gap between my thigh and Jakub's.

"Are you getting excited? It's been a while for you," says Rafe, stretching out his legs before him.

No, it hasn't been a while. It's been since last night. So I guess Jakub hasn't told Rafe we slept together.

"Do you have a plan in mind?" Rafe continues.

Is he seriously giving Jakub dating advice right now? Am I going to have to listen to them discuss what Jakub and Jenna should do together? I mean, I want to pretend last night never happened, but this is going a little beyond what I'd had in mind.

"Not sure if it's a plan," Jakub sways his head back and forth, uncertain. "But I have a color palette in mind at least."

Rafe nods. "I get that. I always have a vague sense of the type of wood I want to work with first too. And then the wood tells me what it wants to be. I'm sure the colors will speak to you when it's time."

This is the most confusing dating advice I've ever heard. Confusing enough that I'm tempted to ask them what they're talking about, despite really not wanting to hear the details of Jakub's relationship with Jenna.

"Yeah, between the adrenaline of creating and the pressure of the timer, something will happen. Who knows if it'll be worthwhile though." Jakub reaches out to stroke a finger between Lucy's eyes and up over her head between her ears.

Lucy leans her head into Jakub's touch and girl, same. That's the exact same finger Jakub used to touch me, and I swear I leaned into his touch exactly the same way.

"Well, I'll be there cheering you on," says Rafe. "Sera, you want to come?"

Rafe is going to go watch Jakub's date? What the hell kind of weird-ass date is he going on? I'm so lost that it takes a moment before I realize the more important part of Rafe's question. Did Rafe just ask me to also go watch it? Did Rafe just ask me out?

"Sure?" Whatever my plans are, I'll cancel them.

Now Rafe looks confused by my confusion. "Wait, you don't know?" He looks at Jakub. "You haven't told her?"

Jakub shrugs, not looking either of us in the eye. "It hasn't come up."

Rafe throws up his hands and mumbles something under his breath. I swear it sounds like he says, "Self-sabotage."

"What hasn't come up?" Clearly I'm missing something. I rest my palm along Lucy's spine, feeling the rumble of her purring under my hand as I look between the guys.

"That Jakub is competing in an art battle this weekend," Rafe says when it's clear Jakub isn't going to answer.

"An art battle? That's a real thing?" I've been in the graphic design industry since college and I've never heard of something like an art battle. It sounds kind of cool. I glance at Jakub, wearing a maroon cardigan over his tan T-shirt, trying to picture him doing any kind of battle, and I just can't see it.

Jakub gestures to Rafe as if to say, see?

"It's definitely a real thing," says Rafe, supportive best friend that he is.

"But art isn't a competition." Real art is a form of expression, not something an artist can win at. Or they can, but only against themselves and their own internal roadblocks.

"Excuse me? Not a competition?" Jakub rounds on me. "Says the person who made a point of doing better than everyone else in class and ensuring the professor held your works up as an example? The person who thinks everyone goes after the job you want like it's some sort of race to the top?"

I turn on the sofa to face him. "You do go after the jobs I want! It's like you do it specifically to antagonize me." He is not getting away with making me look like the bad person here.

"Oh, yeah, because there's no way I would apply for a job just because it was a good opportunity or because I didn't like whatever ad agency I was with at the time," he drawls sarcastically as he also turns on the sofa.

We're face to face, Lucy the line drawn in the sand between us.

"Maybe you're both good artists, but in slightly different ways, with different strengths," Rafe interrupts, his hands out as if placating us.

I'd almost forgotten that he was even here. There's just something about Jakub that pushes all my buttons.

Slowly, I sit back in my seat, turning away from Jakub. He'd invited Rafe over so I could flirt with him, that's who I should be focusing on.

"Jakub is actually a phenomenal painter," Rafe continues, as if he's afraid we'll start fighting again at any moment.

My gaze flicks to where Jakub's fingers are still stroking Lucy between the ears, and I recall the flecks of blue paint I saw on them the other day and remembering that Rafe had said he was working on a painting up in his room. Curse my kindness and respect for boundaries by not snooping.

Since I haven't seen any of his paintings to judge for myself, I don't say anything.

"Would you like to come with me on Friday to watch Jakub compete?" asks Rafe slowly, looking between Jakub and me as if we're going to explode again right here on the sofa.

I want to be over the moon that Rafe just asked me out on an honest-to-fuck date, but it's to watch Jakub. Which is not ideal, as far as dates go. But an art battle does sound fun. I've never been a big painter myself, preferring digital art, but I can still appreciate the medium when others do it. "It doesn't sound like the worst way to spend a Friday night."

"Perfect." Rafe claps his hands together once. "I'll pick you up, the bar that's hosting isn't really known for their parking."

If we're driving together, then he'll also bring me home. That thought alone makes me feel better. We can't have a romantic time in a bar that's crowded with people, but there could be some touching and some flirting, and then something magical could happen between us in the car or as he walks me to the door at the end of the night.

Jakub unmutes the TV, and he and Rafe turn their attention to the hockey game as I let myself drift off into a fantasy about large hands slipping around from behind me to slide under the hem of my shirt in a dark bar, then running along the skin of my midriff and soothing away the discomfort caused by my healing bruise as we watch ultramarine paint spattering over a canvas.

Chapter Fifteen

I climb into Rafe's truck on Friday night, telling myself that the night can only get better from here. What kind of guy picks a woman up for a date by texting her *"I'm in the driveway"*? He didn't even get out to open the door and help me into his truck. We could have had one of those romantic moments where he wraps his hands around my waist and lifts me up. Then I'd turn to slide onto the seat, our eyes would meet, and bam, he'd realize I'm the love of his life.

Instead, I'm pulling myself up into this thing on my own and trying to fan my skirt out around me attractively as I settle in the passenger seat. It's not even a bench seat, so I can't accidentally slide over and sit pressed up against him when we go around a turn a little too fast.

"Are you excited to finally see Jakub's art?" asks Rafe, putting the truck in reverse and pulling out of my driveway before I've even shut the door all the way.

He even uses the backup camera and mirrors instead of hooking his arm over the back of my seat to look where he's going like they do in the movies.

"I mean, we were in the same program at school, I've seen his stuff," I say dismissively. No way am I going to let

Jakub become the main topic of conversation for my first ever date with Rafe. "But I'm definitely curious to see what an art battle entails. And, of course, I'm looking forward to spending time with you."

"You'll love it. Competitive and artistic. Should be right up your alley," says Rafe. "And hey, thank you again for letting Jakub move in with you. If he hasn't told you, I know he's really appreciative."

Forcing cheer into my voice even as I clench my jaw, I say, "Glad to help."

"I'm not sure either of us would have lasted long with him crashing on my sofa." Rafe chuckles. "So when I saw you at Rowan's party and remembered you'd just bought a house, I figured what the hell, why not take a chance and ask?"

"You never know until you ask." We need to talk about anything other than Jakub. We're already going to see him for our date, we shouldn't talk about him the entire drive too. "You know, I don't think I've ever seen your place."

"It's tiny, barely enough room for me, but I like it that way. Lots of woods around too, which is nice."

Rafe shoots me a smile like he didn't just basically tell me he's happy living alone. Then what are we even doing on this date? If he's got no plans to share a living space with someone else, it stands to reason that he's not looking for a relationship. I keep the smile plastered on my face, fragile though it may be, and make a noncommittal sound.

"That's why I couldn't have Jakub stay with me for more than a week or so. Not that I'm complaining about him crashing with me." Rafe shakes his head. "He's my best friend and I'd do anything for him. But Lucy needs her space."

Great, more talk of Jakub on this date that Rafe seems determined to ruin.

"That's why I knew he had to come back here," he continues, oblivious to my irritation. "California is big, sure, but when your ex is that big of a bitch, it's not big enough. Besides, all of his friends there had been her friends."

Wait, he'd moved back because of a breakup? Why did I not know this? It had to be serious if he'd leave the state over it.

"Not that they recently broke up," Rafe rushes to add. "It's been about six months, but really, if he moved there for her and hadn't really settled into the place, what's the point in staying there? He can work wherever he wants to, so why not come back here, where he has friends and his art will be appreciated? It just made sense."

Why the hell does it sound like Rafe is trying to reassure me that Jakub's moved on from his ex? This is officially the weirdest date I've ever been on, and we're only now parallel parking at the venue.

Well, not completely at the venue. Rafe wasn't lying when he said the parking is bad here. We now have to walk almost two blocks to the bar, he tells me.

"I can't wait for you to see Jakub in action," says Rafe, coming around the front of his truck to join me on the sidewalk. I didn't even bother waiting to see if he'd open the truck door for me. The way this night is going, I'd have been waiting forever. "He's an amazing painter in general, but it's wild how he can make something so simple have so much emotion in such a short amount of time." He shakes his head. "That's why he does so well at these art battles."

Is he really going to continue this ridiculous praise of Jakub the whole walk? I get it. Jakub is a good painter. He's got friends who like him and want the best for him. I didn't know about his art or his ex-girlfriend, but we're not friends, so I don't need to know all of this. Maybe Rafe is hoping we'll become friends? After all, if Jakub is his best friend, and this night turns into more than a single date, Rafe is going to want me to be friends with his best friend.

It occurs to me as we approach the bar that Rafe didn't try to hold my hand or touch me at all even once on the entire walk from the car, and I wonder if he's just really bad at dating. Maybe that's why he's perpetually single even though he's so hot and such a nice person. Maybe he goes on first dates and spends the whole time talking about other people and not touching the woman, and they all get annoyed and don't want to go out with him again.

He does open the door to the bar for me, at least. Well, okay, I kind of dart in when he opens it before he can go in himself, but it still counts.

"Looks like we're just in time," he says, pointing to the stage, where a woman with short, spiky blond hair and a swishy black skirt is setting up blank canvases on easels.

Jakub is hovering at the bottom of the stage stairs with a few other artists. I can tell by the way they're dressed, mostly in retro or quirky styles. Which makes Jakub look out of place among them. They must be getting ready to go up and start this battle soon.

"Let's get a drink and then we can find someplace to sit." I lead the way over to the bar, lest Rafe decide he wants us to go down and talk to Jakub before the competition.

It's crowded in here. How do so many people know about art battles, but I had no idea they were a thing until a few days ago?

It's so loud we have to yell over the bar to order our drinks. I pull out my card to start a tab, and Rafe doesn't stop me or offer to pay for us both. Which is fine, I don't expect men to pay for me, but it's always nice to have the person who asked you out offer to pay for the date.

"Looks like there are seats in the back there." I gesture with my white wine to the back corner. It's loud in here, but we might be able to have an actual conversation if we sit there. Hopefully a conversation about anything other than Jakub.

"Actually, let's go stand at the front. I want to make sure Jakub knows we're here to support him and his art. Besides, you haven't seen him compete yet, and you're sure to be impressed." Rafe leads the way through the crowd without waiting for me to agree.

With a sigh, I follow him. Does Rafe not understand that this is a date and we should be spending our time getting to know each other better? We can support his friend without having to make the entire evening about only him.

Jakub is surrounded by other people so we can't get anywhere near him, thank fuck. Who knew he had so many friends here?

"I want to wish him luck before the competition," says Rafe, so he leverages his size and forces his way through the crowd. I don't follow. I'm here for Rafe, not Jakub.

Rafe reaches Jakub and leans in for a bro hug, then keeps his face close enough to Jakub's that they can and hear each other over the noise of the crowd. He must say my name, because Jakub's eyes immediately search the crowd and lock on mine. The room seems to quiet for a moment when we make eye contact, and my stomach does a flip. I feel unsettled, like I'm about to go on for a bout that I'm not quite prepared for.

I raise my wine glass in acknowledgement and look away. I feel exposed, like he's caught me doing something I shouldn't be, and I don't like it.

"Welcome back!" says the woman, stepping up to the mic on stage. "Or welcome, for anyone just now joining us. I'm Jenna, and I run Creative Capital."

Oh, so this is the woman who has been messaging and

calling Jakub. I'm relieved to put a face to the name, and to learn she's the event organizer, because it means I can stop wondering about her. Although she's very pretty, and just because she's the event organizer doesn't mean Jakub isn't also hooking up with her.

I don't think I like how peppy she is.

"We're just getting ready to start round two of our qualifiers to determine who will compete for Art Battle Champion Portland," she continues. "Franklin was our round one winner, so let's find out who's going to challenge them. As with round one, the theme for these pieces is Space. Are you ready to see these local artists compete?"

The crowd cheers, whoops and shouts of "Hell yeah!" filling the bar, and four artists, including Jakub, file up onto the stage to stand in front of their easels. Jenna introduces each one to the crowd, reading out a little bio and description of each artist, and when she gets to Jakub, she chuckles.

"Last but not least, we have Jakub Lattner, newly returned to the Portland art battle scene and self-described cat dad," she announces. The crowd laughs and Jakub grins and waves, and then Jenna calls for one more round of applause for all the artists as they prepare to get started.

Rafe finally manages to squeeze his way back through the crowd to me. "You're in for a real treat."

"I'm sure," I squeak out, and sip my wine. It's weird to see Jakub up on stage with a whole room of people cheering for him. "So how does this work exactly, did we miss round one?"

"Round one happened before we got here, yeah, but it's a whole different group of people. They have two rounds and the winners of each compete to be the overall winner." Rafe shakes his head and sips his own beer as he stares up at the stage. "I can't believe you've never been to an art battle before."

As Jenna starts the timer and we watch the artists begin painting, I agree with Rafe. Why didn't I know about this before? The artists are working not just with acrylic paints, but also with pastels and pens, and one has watercolors—none of which I use, but they're amazing. I'm completely focused on watching their hands fly across the canvases, trying to capture the image in their heads in the tight time frame of only twenty minutes. All of the pieces are good, but my eyes keep returning to Jakub's.

His paints all set out in an exact order. His lines are bold and confident. It's his colors though, that are the surprise. His clothing has always been muted greys and tans, but the paints he's chosen are bright, flamboyant, nearly neon.

"Wait, is Jakub painting..." I must be wrong. It must be the angle at which I'm standing to the easel.

"Lucy? Yeah, he's been working on an entire series dedicated to her and her antics," Rafe confirms.

"As a tea-drinking astronaut in space?" I'm surprised that Jakub would paint something so whimsical when everything about him has always been so organized and exacting and...well, boring.

Rafe laughs. "Well, not her real, everyday antics. More the things he imagines Lucy wishes she could get up to."

He's not wrong. I've only known Lucy for a short while, but I very much imagine she would dream of flying through space while daintily sipping tea. She's such a lady.

It's almost a shock when the bell rings again, signaling the end of the round.

"Thank you, artists," calls Jenna, stepping back up to the microphone, and all of the artists immediately step away from their easels. "Now, for the audience interaction part. Scoring."

Jenna moves along the stage, pointing at one canvas after another, listening and analyzing the roar of the crowd. One artist did a landscape with forests and crashing waves, another painted a child with their arms out spread, and the third, a head opening up with shapes escaping done in oil pastels, gets the loudest applause from the crowd. When she finally gestures to Jakub's, Rafe cheers and hollers so loud I worry for my eardrums. Even I cheer for him, partly because I know Rafe wants me to and partly because his piece is truly my favorite of the four.

Finally, she announces, "Looks like we have our round two winner! Jakub will go up against Franklin after a ten-minute intermission."

"So what do you think?" asks Rafe, watching the crowd milling around as we wait for the final round.

"It's not bad." I'm reluctant to admit just how impressed I am. I want Rafe to think he planned a good date, because this is pretty cool, but I also don't want to admit that Jakub is truly talented. Although considering all the people here who love his art, it's the truth, whether I want to admit it or not.

Rafe raises an eyebrow at me, and I roll my eyes.

I laugh. "Fine, this whole art battle thing is pretty awesome."

"And?" he presses.

"And Jakub is a decent painter," I begrudgingly admit.

Rafe snorts a laugh into his beer. "Close enough."

"Why does it matter so much to you if I like his work?" I watch Jakub onstage, prepping his paints and a fresh canvas for the next round alongside a person in a long skirt and a knitted vest who I assume must be the round one winner.

My question seems to catch Rafe off guard, and he takes a moment before answering.

"He's my best friend," he says, slowly as if thinking over each word. "And I want to support him in any way I can."

I guess that makes sense. Rafe wouldn't want to date someone who hates Jakub any more than I'd date someone who hates Daphne. We're best friends and that means we're a package deal. It's probably the same for Rafe and Jakub. So if this is a test to see if he wants to take me out again, I guess I'd better recommit to that whole coexisting-peacefully-with-my-roommate thing.

"Well, I'm curious what Jakub is going to paint Lucy doing for the final round." It's not necessarily a compliment of his work, but I'm not quite ready to admit how much I liked the first painting, or how interested I am in the next one.

Although if I were being completely honest with Rafe, I'd have to admit that I'm very interested. Jakub's painting is not only technically perfect, but it's also arresting. One of the types of pieces that it's hard to look away from, and even harder to walk away from. It would call everyone in a museum room over to it.

"I am too. I wonder what they're going to announce as the theme."

"They haven't announced it yet?"

"Not for this round. They give the artists the theme for the first round ahead of time so they can prep reference photos, but for the final round, they have no idea what the theme is until just before the timer starts," Rafe explains.

The idea of having to produce something worthy of the eyes of so many people without being able to think about it ahead of time is terrifying. Give me women barreling down on me in skates any day.

"Are we ready to learn who our Art Battle Champion is?" Jenna calls out over the microphone.

"It's Jakub!" Rafe yells back.

The crowd erupts in laughter, and even Jenna can't help but join in. But Jakub, he's not laughing at all. He's completely stoic, his gaze trained on me and Rafe out in the crowd.

Well, I assume it's on both of us, but I swear it feels like he's staring into my soul.

"Very funny, but let's let the artists compete first," Jenna tells Rafe, wagging a finger in his direction. "Our theme for this final round...is 'love'." Then she rings the bell for the competition to start, and the timer begins to count down.

"Oh man, Jakub should have held off on painting Lucy until this round. Or do you think"—I turn to Rafe—"is he allowed to do two paintings of his cat in the same battle?"

"I don't know if there's a rule about that. I'm not sure what he's going to do," he replies, but he's not meeting my eye.

There's something cagey about the way he's refusing to look at me. If I didn't know better I'd think he's hiding something, but given that he's now eye flirting with Jenna, who is standing off to the edge of the stage, I suspect that is more likely the reason, and a swell of irritation surges through me. Rafe hasn't exactly been the picture of chivalry on this date, but I never would have thought he'd be openly making eyes at another woman right in front of me.

Before I can call him out, though, Jakub applies the first swath of paint. Vermillion.

His painting in the previous round was all confident lines, and I could clearly see his organized process as he worked. But this round, Jakub is chaos. I forget about Rafe and Jenna and just watch him work, drawn in like a moth to a literal flame as an inferno develops on his canvas.

Everything around me fades away. Nothing exists in this bar but me and Jakub and this painting.

If he's this good of a painter with a theme that he was given only moments ago, what could he do with a brief that he has a couple of hours or even days to mull over? And to execute it so quickly with this much skill is more impressive than even his round one painting. A tiny voice in the back of my head whispers that this is the reason he got hired for all those jobs I applied to. It wasn't that I was bad at graphic design or that he had an in with the company, it's this right here. While I'm talented, he's a savant.

I would buy anything this painting is advertising. The image blossoming on the canvas is terrifying and compelling, and I want it.

The faint image of a woman reaches out from within the flames, beckoning the viewer into the blaze. Or maybe she *is* the glowing flames, licking at everything around her.

This is what he sees as love?

The bell ringing to signal the end of the final round startles me, and I look around quickly. If Rafe was trying to talk to me, I didn't hear a word he said, so involved was I in Jakub's painting process. But he's still eye-fucking Jenna, so I suspect I didn't miss anything.

Jenna crosses back to the center of the stage as the crowd murmurs. "Huge thank you for everyone coming out tonight to support our local artists. Please follow all of them on their socials and check out their work," she says. "And thank you to all of our artists for competing tonight. It's not an easy thing to come out here onstage and put yourself out there like this, so let's give a hand to all of tonight's competitors."

The crowd offers a general round of applause, but they're clearly anxious to cast their votes for the winning painting.

"And now for the moment you're waiting for," Jenna says, acknowledging the tension in the room. "Let's see who won, shall we?"

She moves to Franklin's beautifully executed portrait of two wrinkled hands, clasped together, and the crowd applauds enthusiastically. But when she crosses to Jakub's easel, they go absolutely wild.

Jakub offers a half smile in response, and when Jenna announces him as the winner, I expect him to let it turn into the real thing, but he doesn't. It's a shame, because while the subdued version of his smile is nice, I realize that since he's been back in town, I haven't seen him truly smile. He's a good-looking guy, I'm finally willing to admit, and I bet with an honest-to-fuck grin of delight, he'd be gorgeous.

He turns to offer his competitor a handshake and some words I can't make out from here, probably something nice about their painting, and all the artists from his earlier round flood the stage to congratulate him, along with a group who I assume to be the first-round artists.

"I told you he'd win," Rafe says into my ear, leaning close so I can hear him over the din of conversation that's sprung up around us. "What do you think of his painting?"

He smells like he always does, clean and forest-y, and I wait for the zing in my belly that usually comes with him being so close to me. But this time, probably because of all the people around, there's no zing.

I look sideways at Rafe, sure that whatever I tell him, he'll report back to Jakub. It's what I would do for Daphne.

"It deserved to win." It's the best compliment I can give, and a subtle acknowledgement that Jakub was worthy of every job he got that I didn't, as much as it pains me to admit it.

"Let's go congratulate him." Rafe is already winding his way through the crowd to meet Jakub as he steps off the stage. He holds his arms wide and folds Jakub into a hug. "Congratulations, man."

"Thanks for coming out," Jakub says to him before turning to where I'm hovering awkwardly behind Rafe. "You too."

"No worries." I shrug, downplaying my presence. "It was interesting."

Part of me is screaming, *Tell him how good his pieces were!*, but I can't. Not right now, anyway. I still need to process my feelings about them, especially the second one.

"Yeah." Jakub looks around the room like he's not sure what to do with himself. "Well...I guess I'm going to go clean my brushes and collect my things."

He holds up a hand in a small wave of acknowledgment at a few people who congratulate him as they walk by.

"Oh, if you're heading home, would you mind giving Sera a lift? I need to have a chat with someone," says Rafe, already glancing over to the bar.

I follow his gaze and sure enough, there's Jenna, leaning against the bar and watching us.

I can't believe this. Is he seriously ditching me mid-date to go chat up some other woman? How tacky can one man be?

But then, this whole evening has been kind of a bust. And if Rafe doesn't want to continue hanging out with me, then I don't want to force myself on him.

However, maybe Jakub wants to stay and hang out with friends or drink. He just won his competition, he shouldn't have to feel pressured to take me home instead.

"It's fine," I say. "I can call Daphne, or get a rideshare."

There's a moment of awkward silence between the three of us, and I wave my hand uselessly through the air. "Really. It's fine." It's not fine. I'm annoyed, and I'm sad, and in a few minutes those two things are going to coalesce into anger. Or tears. I need to get out of here before that happens. I hold up my phone. "I'll see you guys later."

"I can take you," says Jakub, looking between Rafe and me. I can't read the expression on his face, and I'm beginning to realize that this is often the case these days.

Rafe, on the other hand, looks delighted, and claps Jakub on the shoulder. "Thanks, man." Over his shoulder, he says to me, "I'm glad you came out tonight. I'll see you later," and before he's even finished speaking, he's striding over to where Jenna is waiting at the bar.

Now in addition to annoyed and sad, I'm also humiliated. Not just by Rafe's dismissal of me, but because Jakub witnessed it.

"Seriously, you should stay and hang out with your friends," I tell him, willing my voice to sound normal and not like I'm about to cry. "I'm sure they all want to buy you a drink and congratulate you. I can get a ride."

"It's no problem, I want to go home and check on Lucy anyway," says Jakub, tilting his head to indicate I should follow him. He climbs the steps to the stage, but the last thing I want is to stand up in front of everyone here when I'm feeling this raw and exposed, so I lean against the stage, resting my elbows on it. I'm glad I wore a long-sleeved top. The sleeves will get dusty from their contact with the stage, but at least I'm not touching it with bare skin.

Silently, I watch Jakub pack up his paints and brushes. There are no wasted movements. In his process Everything is efficient and methodical.

When his supplies are all tucked safely into their bag, he jogs back down the steps to where I'm waiting.

"What about your paintings?" I ask. Surely he's not going to leave those gorgeous pieces here at the bar.

"We're all picking them up tomorrow since they're not fully cured," he tells me as he leads me through the crowd.

"Besides, this way they're still on display for everyone to view, and hopefully it'll entice people who get here later tonight to come to the next art battle."

"Oh, okay." He's got a good point. If I showed up for a night out with friends and saw all these art pieces, they'd get my attention. And when I learned they were the product of an art battle, I'd want to attend the next one and see what it's all about.

I pause and glance back at the stage. Jakub patiently holds the door as I take one last look at the paintings. Lady Lucy sipping her tea among the stars and the woman on fire are bright under the stage lights, and it's almost like they're trying to tell me that even though my date with Rafe was a disappointment, I shouldn't wallow for too long because there's still so much out there waiting to surprise me.

Chapter Sixteen

I'm very proud of myself for only looking back at the paintings and not searching the crowd for a last glimpse of Rafe. I keep my eyes trained on Jakub's back as I follow him down the sidewalk to his car, and when he bends to stow his paints in the trunk I can't help but notice that he's got a really nice butt.

What am I doing, checking out Jakub Lattner's ass after being ditched by Rafe Kestral for some other woman? I should be nursing my hurt feelings, not objectifying my roommate, whom I don't even particularly like. But I do feel a small stab of petty amusement when I realize that actually, Jakub's butt is every bit as cute as Rafe's. Maybe even cuter.

Take that, Rafe.

Jakub closes the trunk and I snap my gaze to my adorable ankle boots so he doesn't realize I was looking at him. He moves to the passenger side and opens the door for me.

"I didn't need you to do that for me," I tell him as I slide into my seat.

"I know." Jakub closes my door and then rounds the front of the car to the driver's side.

I'm hit with two memories—one of myself trying to appear ladylike as I hoist myself into Rafe's truck earlier this evening, and the other of me drunkenly telling Jakub that I don't need him to open the door for me. My eyes burn with the threat of tears as I realize that all he's doing is giving me a ride home, and he's treating me more like someone he's on a date with than Rafe did on our actual date. I'm pretty sure the universe is laughing at me at this point.

The silence in the car is overwhelming. What kind of person doesn't have their radio on when they're driving?

"Thanks for driving me home," I tell the passenger window. The anger I expected over Rafe ditching me in front of Jakub never came. Only more sadness and embarrassment. If I look over and see pity on Jakub's face, I'll give in to the tears that are simmering just under the surface, and I cannot handle the mortification of him seeing me cry on top of everything else.

"It's not a problem," he says softly. Then, sounding more upbeat and normal, he adds, "We're going to the same place anyways, right?"

"Yeah." I don't want to be reminded. I had started this evening hoping I'd be sleeping at Rafe's place tonight. Not coming back to my own house in the passenger seat of Jakub's Prius.

He pulls into the driveway behind my hatchback, and I barely wait for him to park before I'm climbing out and running up the porch steps. I can hear him grabbing his paints out of the trunk as I unlock the front door. I don't even want to text Daphne to tell her what happened. I'm just ready to be in my bed, alone, and have this day be over.

As soon as the door opens, Lucy comes flouncing down the stairs and beelines right past me to greet her dad as he comes in behind me. Wonderful. Even the cat is passing me over in favor of someone else tonight.

I can't even get mad when I spot the little indentation where Lucy has been sleeping on my covers all day. It's my own fault for forgetting to close my bedroom door again.

I close it now, and mope my way through my bedtime routine.

I'm about to slide in between the covers and queue up a sad movie on my phone to wallow in my feelings when there's a knock on my bedroom door. I wait, not sure I want to open it. I don't really need any more embarrassment for tonight.

Jakub knocks again. "Sera?"

"What is it?" I open the door just a little, enough for me to peek out but not for him to see in.

"Um," Jakub glances at a spot just above my head, and I fight the urge to turn around to see if he can see into my room. "It might storm tonight. Maybe we should sleep downstairs?"

Of course it's going to storm. Because my life couldn't get worse right now.

"Okay," I sigh, and turn away from the door to gather up my pillow and check my phone. It's odd that Daphne hasn't texted to let me know about the impending storm. Although if she's in the middle of a competition, she wouldn't stop to check the weather and text me, it would ruin her time.

I turn back to my door and am surprised to see that Jakub is still in the hallway, waiting. He didn't take advantage of the open door to come in and look around, and he didn't disappear off to the basement on his own. He's just...waiting for me and respecting my space. Huh.

I follow Jakub downstairs to the basement, stopping short when I see that the pull-out bed is already set up. He set the bed up by himself? I can't decide if that's sweet, that he went to find clean sheets and prepped the room knowing I'd want to sleep down here if there's bad weather, or if, given that the last two times we slept here he got lucky, I should be annoyed that he's making it so easy for a repeat interaction.

Deciding I'm too drained to care, I toss my pillow on the bed next to his and look around.

"Where's Lucy?" It's odd that Jakub would come down to set up the bed but didn't bring his cat down.

"Oh, uh, right." Jakub jogs back up the stairs and returns a few minutes later with Lucy in his arms. "Wouldn't, uh, want her up there alone tonight. With a storm, and all."

He's acting weird, and I don't have the mental energy for it right now. I just want to be sad and go to sleep. Jakub can do whatever he wants.

I slide under the covers, hugging the edge of the mattress. I'm so over today that I can't even muster any fear for the oncoming storm. I'm sure it will hit once the wind and thunder start up, but right now, I'm too drained to care much.

Lying here in the dark, I listen for the storm to start, but it's quiet outside. I don't even hear Jakub playing on his phone over on his side of the bed. It's as silent down here as it is out there.

After a few minutes, he rolls over and places a hand on my upper arm, letting it rest there for a moment. Normally I'd pull away, and part of me wants to, but it's been a long, tough night and his touch is grounding. I let out a breath and begin to relax.

He must mistake my sigh for one of irritation, because he lets out a deep one of his own and starts to roll away. I reach up a hand to catch his before he lets go of me completely. Maybe I don't want to be alone right now.

Maybe I need comfort in another warm body to make me forget everything.

Is it necessarily fair, to use him like this when I'm hurting over the way his best friend treated me tonight? No. I know that. But I'm pretty sure neither of us is under any illusion about what this is between us. He's using me for sex as much as I'm using him for it. It just that this is the first time I want it to distract me from feeling sad rather than scared.

I can feel Jakub still beneath my touch. And then he rolls back to me, sliding his arm down around my waist and embracing me beneath the covers. Our bodies press tight against each other, his front to my back. But he makes no other move.

Swallowing hard, I trail my hand down his arm until it covers his own, then I show him where I want him to touch me.

"Please," I whisper when he still doesn't do anything. I want him to help me forget how bad today was, even if only for a few minutes. I need him to take control. I don't have it in me to call the shots tonight.

"Are you sure?" Jakub asks, still unmoving.

"Yes." I squeeze his hand, pressing it hard against my body where I'm aching to be touched.

"Then strip," he orders.

I freeze, sure I misheard. That isn't how we do this. When Jakub and I hook up, neither of us verbalizes anything, and no one removes any more clothing than is strictly necessary. It's easier to pretend it never happened that way.

"You heard me," he says, drawing away. "If you want this, take off your clothes."

I'm a little bit tempted to do as he says. The fumbling under each other's clothes has an illicitness to it that's appealed to me up to now, but maybe tonight I don't want to feel like we're each other's dirty little secrets. I thought I wanted him to make me feel better about the way things went with Rafe the way he's made me feel better about the storms, but maybe that isn't what I need. Maybe I need to feel him completely, to let him touch me unhindered by clothing. Maybe if I give him full access to my body, he'll be able to make me feel even better than he has already.

But after the way Rafe acted on our date, I'm not feeling particularly trusting. If I'm the only one of us who's naked, Jakub could use that against me somehow, and then I'd be even worse off than I already am.

"You too," I tell him. It comes out sounding like a challenge.

"Okay."

The mattress shifts as he tosses the blankets off and begins to shuck his shirt and pants. The soft sound of fabric hitting concrete tells me he's holding up his end of the bargain, so I suppose I should as well.

I shimmy my shorts and panties down my legs and kick them out from beneath the covers, then tug my shirt over my head and toss it to the floor as well.

It's dark in the basement, but he must hear my clothes hit the floor the way I heard his because he's back, his chest flush against my back, his hand gliding over my skin. He cups my breasts in his palms and feathers kisses along my shoulder and the side of my neck. I angle my chin to give him better access as the flutters begin in my belly.

I reach back between us and wrap my hand around his stiffening cock.

I give him an experimental tug, and his answering groan shoots straight to my core, making my pussy clench with anticipation. I repeat the motion, following it up with a slight roll of my palm over the head of his cock, smearing the pre-cum that's beaded at the tip. By the third stroke, Jakub is dragging his own cock in and out of my fist.

"Tease," whispers Jakub against my shoulder blade. "Two can play at that game."

I do love games.

With one hand, Jakub rolls the bead of my nipple between two fingers while the other slips between my thighs, which automatically open to him. My body remembers exactly how good he can make me feel.

I'd be embarrassed about how wet Jakub has already made me if it weren't such a relief to have him slide a finger inside me. He presses in all the way and then immediately retreats, only to slide in again with a second finger, stretching me as he scissors them against my inner walls until I'm squirming.

Then he adds his thumb, pressing it against my clit.

The pressure inside me builds, but as soon as I'm about to ease into the orgasm, Jakub pulls his fingers away and begins kneading my thighs and ass and hip.

Oh, fuck that. If he's going to edge me, then I'm going to edge him right back. He was right about one thing, two can play this game.

My hand is still around his cock, trapped between our bodies, and I slide it along the shaft again, letting my thumb slide over the slit to collect more pre-cum. He groans again, thrusting against me.

"Roll over," he commands, teasing openmouthed kisses over my shoulder. I roll forward onto my stomach, but he tugs my hips back toward him. "This way."

I can't. If we have sex face-to-face, even though it's too dark to see each other, that's opening up a level of intimacy I don't want. This is supposed to just be about physical pleasure. We're not supposed to have to think about who it's coming from.

"No."

"Well. All right, then." He begins to pull away, back toward his side of the bed, but I'm still holding his cock, and I don't let go.

No way am I letting him stop now, not when my body got a taste of his fingers inside me and is now begging for his cock next.

"Easy there," Jakub says. "Use your words."

"Can't you just…" No, if I ask, it'll be easier for him to deny me. "I want you to fuck me from behind again." I stroke him again for good measure, and he twitches in my palm.

Jakub chuckles, his breath fanning against my skin. "You do have a great ass."

As if to emphasize his point, he cups my ass, separating my cheeks, and for a moment I wonder if he's going to ask to fuck me there this time. Would I let him? I've never done that before, but something tells me that if Jakub edges me one more time, I just might agree to try it tonight.

"Fine, get up on your knees." Jakub slaps my ass playfully as he shifts to kneel over me.

As I push up onto my hands and knees, I expect to hear the condom wrapper opening, but instead I just hear the blankets being arranged and Jakub moving around behind me. I'm about to ask him what he's waiting for when he reaches around me to grab the fronts of my thighs, tugging my knees wider apart, and then places a palm between my shoulder blades and presses my top half down onto the mattress.

I'm grateful for the darkness cloaking us so that he can't see me, ass up and knees wide, presented before him.

Again, I listen for the sound of the condom wrapper, but instead Jakub places his hands on the backs of my thighs, using his thumbs to spread my pussy lips wide. Then he flicks his tongue against my center heat, and I cry out in surprise, burying my face in my pillow to muffle my moans as he gets to work.

Jakub dives in like a man starved, dragging the flat of his tongue through my folds. He fucks me with his tongue, unfolding it inside me to press against my inner walls, mimicking what he did with his fingers. It feels incredible, but it's not enough. My hips shove back against his face of their own volition, seeking more—more depth, more stretch, more than a tongue is capable of providing.

But instead of sheathing his cock in my pussy like I want, Jakub continues working me with his mouth, switching tactics to focus on my pulsing clit. He blows a breath of cool air on it, flicks it with the tip of his tongue, then closes his lips over it and sucks deeply before doing it all again.

I can feel my orgasm building, and I'm convinced that Jakub is going to pull back and deny me again. I try to hide how close I am, pressing my face into the pillow again until I can hardly breathe.

Finally, Jakub stops teasing me. He sucks my clit into his mouth while simultaneously flicking it with his tongue, and I tumble over the edge into bliss, lifting my face from the pillow to gasp for air as waves of sensation course through me.

Jakub moves away and, finally, there's the crinkle of a wrapper and then he's behind me again, the head of his cock pressed against my opening. My ass is still in the air as he slides home in one smooth thrust, and if I weren't so buzzed on pleasure, I'd feel self-conscious. But as he begins to move, gripping my hips with those dexterous artist's fingers as he pumps his length through my orgasm-slick heat, all I can think is that I'm glad he agreed to drive me home tonight, because no rideshare would feel this good.

Chapter Seventeen

I'm making coffee as quietly as possible again, but I'm obviously not quiet enough because Jakub comes up from the basement dressed only in boxers, rubbing the sleep out of his eyes.

The front of his boxers are tented by a morning hard-on. If I'd stayed downstairs in bed, would he have woken me up with another fuck?

I shouldn't be going there. He's my roommate, and I have a crush on his best friend. Or at least I did. After Rafe treated me like I was barely even his friend last night, I'm not feeling so favorably toward him. I am not going to allow myself to crush on a guy who would flirt with another woman when we're supposed to be out on a date.

Granted, I did still fuck Jakub even when I thought he might be talking to that Jenna woman. But that's different. He didn't ditch me for her mid-date.

Ugh. I'm not caffeinated enough for this line of thinking.

"Good, coffee." Jakub comes up next to me at the counter and pulls down a mug.

I can't help the way my eyes focus in on the way his

muscles stretch as he reaches into the cupboard. Or how he still smells good even though he just woke up and hasn't showered yet.

He pours coffee into his mug and leans against the counter, doing nothing to hide the way his morning wood lifts the fabric of his boxers from me. If anything, it's almost like he's intentionally displaying it.

For the briefest of moments, I wonder what he'd do if I dropped to my knees before him and tasted him the way he tasted me last night.

What is wrong with me? I cannot actually be thinking about going down on Jakub in the middle of the kitchen. Or at all. I focus on pouring my own coffee, but as I replace the carafe on the burner, I sneak one more glance at his boxers.

Nope, I'm not going there.

I rush to sip my coffee and scald my tongue.

Jakub gives me a weird look over the rim of his mug as he blows on it to cool the surface. The same way he blew on my clit and gave me shivers last night.

"I guess the storm wasn't so bad last night, I don't think I even heard it." I sip my coffee again. It's still too hot, but it's something to do.

That must be why Daphne never texted me. She must have read the radar better than Jakub can.

"Yeah, same." Jakub sips his coffee, makes a face at it, then sips it again.

Did he really just grimace at my coffee? I get that it's not as good as his, not that I'm going to admit that out loud, but it's not that bad.

Lucy enters the kitchen through the basement doorway and stretches right at the top step.

"Biiiiig stretch," says Jakub. "Should I get you some fresh water to have with your breakfast?"

Jakub sets his mug on the counter to pick up Lucy's

water dish. He carries it to the sink as Lucy prowls over to her food dish.

Lucy sits regally, waiting. She blinks at me, and I smile into my mug. She really is a very pretty cat.

Once Jakub sets down her water dish, she laps daintily at it before moving over to eat her breakfast, one kibble at a time.

Jakub grabs his coffee mug from the counter and sits down at the table, watching Lucy.

But I'm watching him. The way he sips his coffee, makes a face, and then takes another sip.

He definitely hates my coffee. I should be insulted, but he's not wrong. Whatever magic he uses, his coffee is so much better.

I am, however, a little insulted that he's not even trying to pretend to be polite about it.

I cross to the sink and act like I'm rinsing out my cup, but really, I'm dumping out the remainder. I have plans to meet Daphne in a little bit anyway, I can get coffee then.

Just as I'm about to leave the kitchen, I pause. Should I say something to Jakub about where I'm going or what I'm doing today? We've never done that before, and it's not like we're in a relationship. I don't know if we're even friends. But maybe it would be a nice, roommate-y gesture?

I decide to stop overthinking it and leave him to watch Lucy eat. The swinging kitchen door nearly hits me on the ass on my way out.

The ass Jakub thinks is great.

That thought fills my mind as I shower and dress.

On my way, I text Daphne as I bounce down the stairs.

I glance toward the kitchen when I reach the main floor. Again, I consider going in and saying something to Jakub. His bedroom door was still open when I came out of mine so he must still be in there.

Daphne texts back, *I've just arrived and ordered for us.*

I hurry out the front door and to my car. If Daphne already ordered, I don't want to miss my coffee at its hottest. Even though the minute I arrive, she's going to grill me about my date with Rafe, and I'll have to admit that he ditched me, and I had no choice but to let Jakub make me feel better.

She's never going to let me hear the end of it.

Thank fuck Rafe isn't working this morning. I'm not in the mood to see him.

"Thank you," I murmur as I drop into the chair across from Daphne and bring the mug she slides my way up to my lips like it's an offering.

"Yikes, how terrible was the art battle?" She cups her own mug in her hands and leans back in her chair.

"The art battle itself was great. Interesting even, but the date itself..." I set my coffee mug carefully back in its saucer and rest my head in my hands. How am I supposed to convey the disaster that was last night to my best friend?

"Oh, dear." Daphne puts her hand on my forearm, and when I look up at her she says, "Should we go to a bar instead? Do some shots?"

I can't help but laugh. "It's not even lunchtime. Are you channeling your inner Rowan now?"

She shrugs. "Sometimes his method works."

"Only for a short while, unfortunately." I smile sadly. "At some point I would still have to sober up and see Jakub again."

"Oooh, so he's involved in this disaster too?" she asks, far more giddy about this than she should be.

"Yeah," I grit out. "Rafe started eye-fucking another woman during our date and so when the art battle ended, he straight up asked Jakub to take me home so he could go flirt with her!" I close my eyes and pinch the bridge of my nose. I hate reliving the humiliation of that moment. "He probably took her home too."

Although, I remind myself, even if he went home and fucked Jenna, I fucked his best friend. So we're kind of even.

"Oh. Wow. That's...I'm so sorry. I wouldn't have expected that from Rafe," Daphne replies after a moment in which she just stares blankly at me as she wraps her head around what I've just told her.

"But that was really nice of Jakub, to take you home. He didn't want to stay and hang out? Oh, how did he do in the battle?"

"He won. Guess he wasn't in the mood to hang out, he said he wanted to get home to Lucy." I wave a hand and pick up my coffee.

"I don't want to talk about it anymore. What were you up to last night? Did you have another puzzle competition? Usually you text me when there's bad weather on the way so I figured you must have been busy." I try not to sound accusatory. It's not Daphne's job to take care of me, even if she does such a good job of it.

"What bad weather? We don't have a storm on the horizon for at least another week."

"But Jakub said..." I trail off. Did I ever even check the radar? Or did I just blindly follow him down to the basement?

"And let me guess, you accidentally fucked again?" Daphne grins like she's about to block out a jam.

"Well, it's not like we're doing it on purpose," I argue. Although I did put his hands on me. And I did take off my own clothes. And I was the one who grabbed his cock.

"Maybe you're not, but have you ever considered that Jakub might be?"

"No way." I shake my head. "Jakub is as annoyed by me as I am by him."

"Maybe he's annoyed because you keep eyeing up his best friend, and never him." Daphne looks serene as she doles out this bit of wisdom.

"I really hope you're wrong." But there's a little voice in the back of my mind telling me that she might be right.

"Are you sure about that?"

I don't have an answer for her. Because if I look back over the last couple of weeks, I have to admit that my feelings toward Jakub have shifted. And not just because of the sex. Living with him, seeing him with Lucy, having him be willing to help me out with Rafe even though he had no reason to...I don't hate him anymore.

I'm not sure I've hated him for a while.

I'm a bundle of nerves. Daphne's suggestion that Jakub might be interested in me has been running through my head all day. I'm not sure how I'm going to focus out on the flat track.

I shake out my limbs. I need to turn all of this broiling uncertainty into aggression and the determination to block out the other team's jammer.

"Matcha Mayhem!"

As soon as they announce my derby name, I bolt out onto the track to do a lap and let the crowd love me.

I'm prepared for Daphne's sign cheering me on, but my eyes slide immediately past her to Jakub. He's not holding a sign, but he is wearing a team T-shirt.

No, not a team shirt. Mine. The one with my name and number.

My mind starts racing faster than my skates. Is that the shirt Jakub bought the last time he was at one of my bouts? Why would he buy my jersey and not a generic team shirt?

Oh god, Daphne might be right. Jakub might very well like me, and for a lot longer than I would have thought too.

We line up for the first jam and it's hard to focus on the jammer coming up behind and blocking them when my eyes keep wanting to search for Jakub in the crowd. Just to double check that he's still here. That it really is my jersey he's wearing. That my brain isn't just addled from so many good orgasms.

But no matter what I do, I can't block him out. Instead, I decide to keep him in mind. Show him just how good of a blocker I am on the track and try to impress him with just how many jams I can stop. He impressed me last night at the art battle, so now it's my turn.

"Matcha Mayhem!" Rowan high fives me as soon as I skate off the track from the last jam of the night. "They're the ones who are in mayhem right now, to come and dare to mess with you!"

"Thanks, Rowan." I'm sweaty and gross and I'm sure my makeup is everywhere. This is not the look I really want Jakub to see.

Huh. Jakub. Not Rafe. That's weird to think about.

It's also weird that I didn't even notice if Rafe was in the stands.

"You looked like you had something to prove tonight,"

says Tegan, toestopping right before she slams into us. "But you don't, you know. You're a badass all on your own."

"I really am, aren't I?" It's not even a question. I fully embodied Matcha Mayhem out on the track tonight. I knew what I wanted and I got it.

Now I'll have to test out my theory for off the track and if I'm right, I'm going to go after what I want there too.

Rowan and Tegan go off to compliment some of the other players. I start to drift toward the locker rooms, but Daphne appears out of nowhere and throws her arms around me.

"Ugh, you stink," she says, scrunching her nose as she disentangles herself from my sweaty body. "But at least you won. Good job."

"Thanks." I sneak a glance at Jakub, who has followed Daphne over. It's definitely my jersey he's wearing. I'll have to ask Daphne later if she realized. Did she already know he'd bought it and hadn't told me?

"Rafe sends his apologies for not making it tonight," says Jakub, sticking his hands in his pockets and looking at me a little too intensely for how sweaty and disgusting I am right now. "Something came up last minute."

"Oh, sure, okay." I'm actually relieved. I think it'll be a while before I can look at Rafe and not relive the way I felt when he ditched me for Jenna.

"Maybe he'll go to the party tonight at Rowan's," suggests Daphne. "Did you need a ride, Sera?"

Daphne never wants to ride together to these parties because she always stays as late as possible. And she knows I have my car here. Why is she being weird? I narrow my eyes at her, and she blinks back at me, the picture of innocence.

"Actually," I glance again at Jakub, wearing my jersey. Seeing him in it makes my stomach flip. "I think I'm just going to go home and have a chill night. What about you, Jakub?"

Just saying his name sends a shiver through me. I can't remember the last time I said it without disdain, if I ever have. We've always bickered and sniped at each other, since we first met back in college. It feels forbidden to talk to him now like we're just two normal people who don't hate each other.

Oh god, did he ever hate me? Or was that entire rivalry one-sided?

He looks as surprised to hear me say his name as I am to have said it. "Oh, uh, I was thinking of just going home too."

I wonder if that was his plan all along, or if he changed his plan because I said I was going home. I'll have to text Daphne later and ask her if he'd said anything about the party beforehand, like during the bout.

"Okay, I'm going to go shower and change." I can't believe I've been chatting for this long while I'm so sweaty and gross. "But I drove here, so no need for anybody to wait around to give me a ride." I turn to Jakub. "I'll see you at home."

Home. I've always thought of it as my house, but now it's home. Our home, even.

Weird.

"Perfect, see you there." Jakub clears his throat. "Good to see you as always, Daphne."

Daphne and I both stand silently as he walks away, and I don't know about her, but I definitely check out his ass. Actually, she better not be staring at his ass.

I glance at her to see, and nope, she's staring at me. Great, here it comes. The grand inquisition.

"So we'll definitely be talking about that later," she says.

"Not now?" I ask hopefully.

She shakes her head. "Rowan just left, so I need to get going too. But have fun tonight," she singsongs.

"You too," I grumble, turning to head into the locker room.

I hope that Daphne has something special happen tonight too, but she'll probably go to the party and just watch Rowan from a corner all night. She knows everyone there, she could talk to someone, but she always just sits and watches. If she would talk to someone—literally anyone, my teammates are always bringing friends to these parties—she could so easily meet someone else, but for some reason she only wants Rowan, even with all of his playboy ways.

Chapter Eighteen

The first thing I notice when I open the front door is the singing coming from the kitchen. I didn't realize anyone would be here except me and Jakub. Unless Jakub's plan to come home was because he had someone coming over.

But then I realize that the voice is his, and he's singing a little song about his cat.

"Lucy in the sky with fishes. Follow her down to the bird feeder. Look at how all the birds fly-i-i-i."

"I didn't realize I was coming home to a concert," I say, walking into the kitchen to see Lucy sitting on one of the pulled-out kitchen chairs and Jakub serenading her, using a wooden spoon as a mic.

Jakub sets the spoon down, his ears turning red. "Well, Lucy likes to feel special."

"That's because she is special." I reach out to pat her head, and she sits up a little more to meet my hand and rub her face against it.

"Very special," agrees Jakub, turning back to the stove. "I made rice and stir fry. Since you went to the track so early, I didn't know if you'd had anything to eat."

"Just a protein bar." My stomach rumbles. It smells so good. "You didn't have to cook for me."

"I have to eat too." Jakub shrugs as he dishes up a bowl and hands it to me before dishing one out for himself. "Do you want to eat in here, or...?"

"Let's watch something." I lead the way into the living room and plop down on the sofa. It'll be easier to spend time with Jakub if I don't have to look him in the eyes the whole time and we have another activity happening at the same time. Less pressure. "Do you like *Brits Who Bake?*"

"I've never seen it." Jakub says, following me into the living room.

"Really? Never? How is that possible?" I look up at him as he sits down next to me. He could have sat in the chair, but he chose to sit on the sofa with me, and I feel a buzz of pleasure as I reach for the remote.

I mentally catalogue the events of the evening that could prove Daphne's theory that he likes me correct. He came to my bout without Rafe. He wore my jersey. He came home instead of going to the party once he heard I wasn't going. He cooked me dinner. And now he's sitting next to me on the sofa instead of in the chair.

It's not nothing, but it's all coincidental. I'm going to need something a little more definitive.

"There has to be a first time for everything," says Jakub as Lucy jumps up to sit on the coffee table. She stares us down, determined to break us so we give her a bite.

"You think I'm weak, but I'm not," Jakub tells her, lifting a forkful to his mouth.

"Speak for yourself." I click on the show icon and set the remote carefully next to Lucy. "She intimidates the fuck out of me."

He nods as he chews. "Lucy does have that effect on people."

The opening credits roll, and I catch myself occasionally glancing over at Jakub to see what he thinks of the show. British people baking in a tent isn't exactly revolutionary television, but it's something I've always found soothing. And right now, with the stress between the thing with Rafe and the possibilities with Jakub, I can really use something familiar and comforting.

"So they're literally just baking," asks Jakub fifteen minutes later, scraping out the last of the rice from the bottom of his bowl.

"Yes, but each week it's a different theme," I explain, pausing the show. I stand and hold out my hand for his empty bowl so I can take both our dishes into the kitchen.

When I come back, Lucy is laid out between Jakub's thighs. She certainly didn't waste any time. I click the remote to turn the episode back on and the three of us watch it to the end.

"Okay, I'll admit it, this is kind of fun," Jakub says. "Maybe one more episode?"

"I could definitely go for one more, and maybe an after-dinner snack," I suggest.

"One snack coming right up," he says. He lifts Lucy off his lap to set her next to him, nuzzling her head as he says, "Not for you though."

Dropping a kiss right on her forehead, he dashes into the kitchen calling over his shoulder, "Don't start the episode until I'm back!"

"I suppose we should be nice, shouldn't we?" I tell Lucy, who leans against me since her dad isn't here.

She's really not bad. I'm not nearly as nervous around Lucy as I was when she first moved in. She might like me too, based on the number of times she's snuck into my room to sleep during the day. Maybe she needs a little bed of her own in there.

Grabbing my phone off the coffee table very carefully so as not to disturb the way Lucy is loafing next to me, I start searching for cat beds that would match the current aesthetic of my bedroom. I'm not buying anything that doesn't go with the rest of the design, even if it is for Lucy.

"Everything okay?" Jakub hovers near the arm of the sofa, holding two small plates aloft.

"Do you like this fleece-lined bed or this felt cave that's shaped like a cloud better?" I turn my phone to show him the screen as he sits down and hands me a plate with grapes and a chocolate chip cookie on it.

"Lucy does love those little caves." He plucks one of the grapes off the stem on his plate and pops it in his mouth.

"This one is shaped like a shark." I show the screen to Lucy. "Do you want to sleep inside a shark?"

"Lucy would probably rather eat the shark," says Jakub, reaching over me for the remote to start the next episode.

"True." I keep scrolling possibilities as the opening music plays. "What about a strawberry, Lucy?"

"Lucy would look great in a strawberry." He reaches over to pet Lucy's head as she stretches out to rest her front paws on my thigh.

Throughout the episode, he keeps petting Lucy, his fingers occasionally brushing against my thigh. I end up holding my breath for nearly half the show, waiting to see if he does more.

It makes it very difficult to focus on the show or eat my dessert.

As the end credits are playing and the screen preps to immediately roll into the next episode, Jakub scratches Lucy's head and asks, "Ready for bed, little girl?"

He stands and gathers our dessert plates.

"I can take care of those," I offer. "You cooked so I should clean." It's only fair.

"Lucy is on your lap," he points out, carrying the dishes into the kitchen. "She isn't ready to move yet."

Okay, that's a fair point. If I move Lucy now, it might make her think I never want her to come snuggle me, and that's not true. Luckily, she moves when her dad comes back into the living room, turning off the lights as he moves through it.

We all troop upstairs. It feels weird to go into our respective rooms like normal. And I'm not sure I'm ready for the evening to end.

Maybe I should test out Daphne's theory.

"There's going to be bad weather tonight, actually," I lie, trying to sound casual. "I'm going to grab my pillow and head downstairs once I'm ready for bed." The implied *if you want to join me* hangs silently between us.

"Oh." Jakub looks surprised, and his hand moves to his pocket where his phone is. "Okay, I'll grab mine too and we can all head down there."

Please don't check your phone, I think to myself as I quickly brush my teeth and change into my cutest sleep shorts and tank. Finally, I hug my pillow to my chest and head out into the hallway where he's waiting in sweatpants and a T-shirt with his own pillow. His hand slides out of his front pocket as though he just replaced his phone in it.

"Did you see the incoming storm on the radar?" I ask, hoping he says he was doing something other than checking the weather. I mean, if he knew I was making it up about the storm, he wouldn't still be following me to the basement, right?

"Yeah, it definitely looks bad," he says. "I'm glad you caught it."

I almost trip over my own feet and fall down the basement stairs. I checked the radar myself as I was brushing my teeth. There's no storm. There's not even a hint of rain anywhere in the forecast.

Daphne was right. She must be. Why else would he be playing along with my obvious lie, unless he's happy for the excuse to spend another night together?

The bed is still disheveled from last night. Normally I'd have come back down to put it away, but I was out with Daphne and then I had to get ready for the bout, so now I'm face to face with the aftermath of our last night together. I throw down my pillow and straighten the blankets on my side as much as possible without looking over at where he's doing the same thing on his side of the bed.

"Where's Lucy?" I ask, keeping up the ruse that there's a storm coming.

"Oh, uh." Jakub slowly climbs onto the bed. "I don't think the storm will be bad enough that she needs to be shut down here. I did leave the door to the basement ajar though. If she does feel unsafe, she can come down."

Well, if I wasn't sure before that Jakub knows I'm making all of this up, I am now. There is absolutely no way he'd leave Lucy alone upstairs if there was even a not-bad storm.

So we're both making up an excuse to sleep down here, but what does that mean? I know what it means on my end —I want to explore these new feelings I'm realizing have been lurking inside me for a while now, feelings I was too stubborn and blind to recognize. But Jakub could just be hoping to get laid again. Even though a few minutes ago I was half-convinced Daphne was right about him having feelings for me, now I'm second-guessing myself. It could well only be that he's horny and figures I am too and that's why I'm faking that there's a storm.

Still, I turn off the light and pad across the concrete floor to climb into the pull-out bed. I can hear Jakub shuffling around, probably taking off his sweatpants. My mind is buzzing, wondering if he took off his shirt too. And maybe his boxers. The idea that Jakub might be completely naked under the covers has me all but running the last couple steps to the bed.

I've barely pulled the blankets over me before he's sliding up against me, his hands kneading my ass and thighs, bunching my shorts in his fists. I reach behind me and my hand lands on bare skin. *So he is naked.* He trails kisses along my shoulder, nudging the strap of my sleep tank off my arm. I'm not sure why we've even bothered with the blankets, because there is clearly enough heat here between us that we don't need any help staying warm.

Jakub hooks his leg over mine, pressing our hips as close as he can get without being inside me. I can feel his cock growing harder against my ass. But he seems more than content to be wrapped around me, his hands roving over my skin, exploring every inch of me in the dark.

When he wraps his arms around me and rolls us so he's on his back and I'm splayed out on top of him, my back still to his chest, I freeze.

"Um, what are you doing?" I'd been expecting him to take me from behind again, because that's what we do, but Jakub seems to be changing the rules. I should be on my front or my side, not awkwardly flopped out on top of him. This is uncomfortable, and I can't even touch him in this position.

Although maybe I was the one who changed the rules when I lied about needing to sleep in the basement.

"It's your turn to fuck me," whispers Jakub, kissing the crook of my neck as he pushes my shorts over my hips. They get caught just under my ass, ensuring that before I can move freely, I'll have to make a decision about whether to pull them back up or take them off. "Don't forget the condom."

He produces one seemingly from nowhere and holds it up in front of me, waiting for me to take the initiative.

I hesitate, then pluck the condom from his fingers. I consider my options. If I do as he's asking, I'll have to maneuver my shorts all the way off, get the condom on him, and get into position.

Or I could set the condom on the mattress, go back upstairs, and pretend this whole thing never happened.

I side-eye Jakub. It's too dark to really see him, but I can feel his hands cupping the sides of my thighs and the hard length of his cock pressed against my ass. I can hear him breathing. Our faces are so close, if I turned my head only an inch or two, I could kiss him.

I suppose I do have a third option, too.

Shoving off my shorts, I push up to sit on Jakub's chest, then shift my knees so I'm kneeling over him. He can stare at my ass in the dark. My focus is on something else entirely. He sucks in a breath as I take him in my hand, stroking my palm over the soft skin of his cock.

I lean down and let my lips part. My tongue flicks out, dragging over the tip of his cock, and I'm immediately rewarded with a groan that makes me feel more badass than any move I've pulled on a flat track. So even though I'd only planned on a taste, I keep going. Flicking my tongue over the slit, swirling it around the head, I drag out Jakub's pleasure and satisfy my own curiosity. I've felt this cock between my thighs and inside my pussy, but now I'm finally able to really hold it between my palms, feeling the heft of it. Solid and silky and the perfect size for my grip.

Jakub reaches down and grabs me around my thighs, dragging me back up his body. I'm not sure what I expected, but it definitely wasn't for him to tug my hips down so I'm sitting on his face.

Jakub's tongue darts past his lips to lick my slit in the same manner I just licked his. I guess our game of teasing has morphed, and two can play this new game too. I wrap my lips around his tip and ease farther down on him, his cock pressing my tongue flat as it fills my mouth. Behind me, his tongue slides into my pussy, teasing at my entrance, but it's not enough.

I pull back, easing Jakub's cock out of my mouth, and he mimics the movement by withdrawing his tongue. I bob down again, and his tongue fills me once more. We work ourselves into a rhythm, my mouth on his cock guiding the rhythm of his tongue.

I'm working myself into a frenzy, desperate for more of him. I hollow out my cheeks as I suck hard, silently begging Jakub to come down my throat, to fill my mouth and coat my tongue. I'm so needy from the tonguefucking he's giving me, if he were to blow one small breath on my clit, I'd combust.

Suddenly, Jakub's hand grips my hair and tugs, pulling me off his cock. I let out a disappointed whimper, which earns me a chuckle.

"I definitely want to come in your mouth at some point, but right now, I want you to ride me," Jakub says through the darkness, his breath warm against my soaked pussy. "So roll on that condom and climb on, Sera."

I'm not sure if it's the authority in his voice or the way it wraps around my name when we're both naked, but I relent. Sitting up more, I unwrap the condom, pinch the tip, and roll it over his shaft.

He gives my pussy one final lick and says, "Now sit on my cock."

There is no question that I'm wet enough to take him.

Just feeling him so hard for me, telling me what he wants me to do to him, is enough to have my heart beating faster and my body aching for him. I was about to climax on his face just moments ago; once I'm stretched around him and he's thrusting into me, I doubt it will take me long at all.

I scoot down Jakub's body to line him up with my entrance. His hands rest on my calves, letting me do the work as he watches through the darkness.

Slowly, I ease down, taking him into me inch by inch. Once he's sheathed to the hilt, I let out a deep breath. The other positions we've tried have all been good, but this one gets him deeper than he's ever been.

I pull off my tank top, and Jakub's hands are on my breasts before it even hits the floor. Leaning back, I rest my palms flat on Jakub's chest for leverage and give my hips an experimental roll. Yes, his tongue was good, but this is even better.

I roll my hips again, and the way he's hitting against my interior walls is going to undo me. I'm not ready for that yet. I want to take the time to fully appreciate the way he fills me, and to tease him until he can't take it anymore.

"Fuck, you feel so good," he groans. His fingers play with my nipples, rolling and pinching them as I ride him.

I lift up, then sink back down onto his cock, squeezing my inner walls to really grip him.

"I want to feel you come on my cock," he whispers, one hand sliding down over my stomach to find my clit.

He glides two fingers over it in tighter and tighter circles until my mind is so focused on his touch that I'm no longer thinking about torturing him with my movements. All I can do is chase the orgasm hovering just out of reach.

Jakub's fingers move even faster until everything in me squeezes in tight and then releases in a glorious burst of pleasure that radiates from his fingers all the way to my own. I can barely stay upright, my hands still pressed against his chest for balance as I ride the waves of climax. Jakub's hands slide to my hips, holding me still as he fucks up into me, racing to his own finish.

He groans and slams me down onto his cock as he comes, his hips thrusting against me once, twice, three times, before he relaxes and pulls me back onto his chest. He rolls us so we're back on our sides, snuggling me tight against him.

He presses a kiss to my hair and sighs deeply, his cock twitching where it's still sunk deep inside me. I think he might whisper goodnight, but I can't be sure, because I'm already tumbling over the edge into sleep, the kind that only comes from every cell in my body being completely wrung out with pleasure.

Chapter Nineteen

Daphne and I carry our coffees over to a table, carefully balancing them to ensure we don't spill any of the life-giving liquid.

"Rowan seemed agitated last night, any idea why?" asks Daphne, sliding into the wooden chair that accompanies the small table.

"No, he seemed fine after the bout." I look longingly over at the floral chairs in the corner, wishing we could be sitting there. I keep one eye on the middle-aged women sitting in them as I turn back to Daphne, ready to jump in and claim the comfy spot the minute they leave. "And I wasn't at the party, but if something happened there, I haven't heard."

"You didn't really miss out on anything," she says, with no excitement in her voice. Then she perks up, wiggling her eyebrows at me as she asks, "How was your night?"

"It was good." I look down at my coffee instead of at her, but I'm sure the way I can't stop smiling gives me away. "We watched *Brits Who Bake*. Can you believe Jakub had never seen it?"

"I'm sure you're showing him a lot of things he's never

seen before." Daphne smirks into her own cup as she leans back into her seat, watching me over the rim.

I stick out my tongue at her and then sip my miel. "I think maybe you were right. Jakub might like me," I admit.

"And how do you feel about him?"

Of course she's not going to let me off the hook. This is the annoying part of having a best friend who knows me so well.

"I...don't hate him."

Daphne laughs. "No kidding. But I bet it's a lot more than that."

Over Daphne's shoulder, I spot a familiar face coming toward us. His shoulders are so wide in his red flannel, there's no way I could miss him, even in a crowd.

"Hi, Rafe," I say loudly to cut off anything else Daphne was about to say.

"Hey, Sera. Hey, Daphne," he says. "Sera, I'm sorry I wasn't able to make it last night. But Jakub said you did great at the bout."

"Thank you." His words fill me with butterflies. Jakub said I was great? Unprompted, or did Rafe ask? "I hope everything was okay."

"Eh." Rafe gives a deep sigh. "It is what it is."

That's...vague. "Well, let us know if you need anything," I offer, not sure if I'm referring to me and Daphne or me and Jakub.

"Oh, hey," he says, changing the subject, "I'm heading up to the lumberjack competition place a few days early to prep for the competition next weekend. Jakub mentioned last week that you thought a cabin in the woods sounded like fun, did you want to come with me? I'm heading out tonight."

"Oh. Wow. Sorry, I can't get the time off work with such short notice." And if our date from the other night is any indication, there's no way I want to be trapped alone in the woods with Rafe for that long. It's disappointing, but I've realized over the last week or so that my crush on him was entirely based on physical attraction, and once I recognized that the crush fizzled out. We just don't have enough in common.

Besides, it's true that there's no way Bartholomew would be willing to let me take a couple days off work with such short notice.

"That's okay. It's probably for the best, anyway," Rafe agrees, nodding in understanding. "The last thing I need is to have Jakub pissed at me."

"What do you mean? Because he already said he'd go?"

"Well, yeah that too."

"Too?" I glance at Daphne to see if she's also confused, but her face is blank.

Rafe seems to be enjoying some sort of private joke with himself. "Yeah. You know."

Has he always been this annoying and I just couldn't see it past the muscles and the dimples? "I really don't, actually."

"It'd kind of break the bro code for me to take you away for a few days in a secluded cabin, right?"

I continue to blink at him in confusion.

"Because he's my best friend? And he's in love with you?" Rafe says.

I don't know what my face looks like right now, but whatever expression I have makes Rafe laugh harder.

And then Daphne joins in.

"Jakub's not in love with me," I say. Sure, he might be somewhat interested in me. A crush. Enough to sleep with me, but sex doesn't equal love.

"He absolutely is," Rafe says, grinning. "Has been for years. He only moved back because of you."

"That's not true."

Rafe nods emphatically. "He was ready to leave California, and I was trying to get him to come back to Portland, but it wasn't until I told him you were single that he finally agreed. He was pissed when I wrangled it so he could move in with you, but I figured if I got you two together in one place for long enough, you might fall for him too. Then he'd be happy, and you'd be happy, and I'd be happy because he wouldn't move away again. I'd like to keep my friend here."

"I...I..." I look to Daphne for help, and thankfully she comes to my rescue.

"I think that's a lot of information for Sera to take in," she tells Rafe, "and we need to discuss it privately."

"Gotcha," says Rafe, slowly backing away. "I'll see you both later then."

As soon as he's out of earshot, I whisper, "What the hell was that?"

My mind is racing faster than a jammer with everything Rafe just admitted. Did Jakub really only move back to town for me? He's in love with me? He's *been* in love with me, for *years*?

"I think that was the cold hard truth." Daphne picks up her coffee mug and sips at it like the entire world didn't just turn upside down right in front of her.

I shake my head, my ponytail whipping back and forth. "It can't be the truth. Jakub can't have come back to Portland just for me. He can't be in *love* with me."

"Maybe he didn't come back just for you," Daphne agrees. "But you were probably a big part of it."

I pin her with a look, my eyebrows drawn together and eyes narrowed. "Did you know about this before now?"

She takes another drink, saying nothing.

"What did you and Jakub talk about at my bout last night?"

"It's a secret."

"Nope. Besties code." No way am I letting her get away with keeping me in the dark on this.

"Fine." Daphne sighs and sets down her coffee on the table. "He basically just asked if I thought he had a chance with you."

"What did you tell him?" I can hear my own heartbeat pounding and feel myself going into fight-or-flight mode. My brain knows there's no reason for it, but my body hasn't seemed to figure that out yet.

"That I think he should go for it." Daphne gives me the sweetest smile, the same look Lucy gives me when she wants me to share a bite of my food. Like she's a perfect little angel baby who's never done anything wrong in her life.

Meanwhile, I feel like the room is closing in on me. I've only barely come to terms with the fact that Jakub probably has a crush on me, and now I'm finding out that he for sure does, and also that it's more than a crush. This is too much pressure. How am I supposed to act normal around him when I get home?

I don't think I've ever closed the front door more gently in my life. If I thought I wanted to avoid seeing Jakub before, it was nothing compared to right now. I need to process. To stare at the ceiling over my bed by myself. Or maybe stare at the wall while sitting in the longest, hottest bath in the world. My thoughts are still lapping each other around the track in my head, and they need to sort themselves out.

I sneak up the stairs, freezing and holding my breath when I step in the wrong place and the stairs let out a squeak. Jakub doesn't appear, but in the silence caused by my stillness I hear his voice upstairs.

Creeping to the top of the stairs, I peek around the corner. Jakub's door is ajar, and he's not using the voice he uses when he talks to Lucy. Does he have someone else in there?

"Bartholomew, I really do appreciate you taking the time to talk to me," says Jakub.

My breath catches in my throat again. He can't be talking to my manager. It must be someone else with the same name.

But how many Bartholomews can there be out there?

"Yes, and you said then I would be overseeing which accounts, exactly?" Jakub pauses, listening to the other end of the call. "Okay, so Livingston Advantage. Any others?"

Nope, that's definitely my boss, because that's the name of the account that I'm directly in charge of at work.

"All right, let me look into those companies to see if they're brands that I'm willing to work with, and I can get back to you soon," says Jakub.

That fucker! I can't believe I thought he liked me. I can't believe I fucked him! Three times! Yet here he is yet again, trying to steal a job from me—and not just any job. No, this time he's going for the job I already have. This is a new low even for him.

The fact that I was dumb enough to sleep with him was probably just the cherry on top of his diabolical plan to ruin my life. He's now fucked me in every way he possibly could, and I bet he's been laughing to his friends about it. He's probably made me the biggest joke in our community.

I dash into my bedroom and text Daphne. *Jakub is a snake in the grass. We hate him.*

Daphne texts me back before I've even closed my bedroom door. *What did he do now?*

He's trying to steal my job! I text back one-handed as I start running the bath.

I add bubbles and undress. I'm sliding into the hot water when Daphne finally texts me back.

Maybe it's a mistake?

No, it was clear as day, I type out. *I heard him say my manager's name, which you know isn't a common one, and then he said "so I'll be overseeing Livingston Advantage." Which is my main account at work. I don't see how I could be misunderstanding that.*

I set my phone to the side and slip down as far into the water as I can while still keeping my nose above the bubbles.

My phone vibrates, but I'm suddenly completely exhausted. I don't even have the energy to lift my arms right now to see Daphne's response.

As I soak, I let myself wallow. I never saw this coming, but I should have. I should have been more suspicious every time Jakub asked me how work was, or brought up an anecdote about a former client that made me open up about something at my job. We weren't bonding, he was mining me for information to steal my job. And then he had the gall to act offended when I accused him of stealing jobs from me in the past.

When the water is barely lukewarm, I run a loofah over every inch of my body, scrubbing free every trace of his touch. What had once been sweet and erotic, I now see as manipulation, lulling me into the false belief that he wasn't taking advantage of me.

Once I pat myself dry, I throw on my comfiest

sweatpants and a tank, then prepare to crawl into bed and wallow some more.

There's scratching at my door. I try to ignore it, but Lucy is persistent. Finally, I slide off the bed and open the door for her. The little white cat sashays into my room, looking distinctly miffed that I'd had the audacity to close the door and even try to keep her out.

She leaps gracefully up onto the bed.

"Well, make yourself at home, why don't you?" I leave my bedroom door ajar so I don't have to get up again if she wants to leave, then stretch out on the bed next to her.

I'd thought she would curl up in her normal spot, but instead she steps right onto my chest and lays down on me like a sphinx, staring down into my face unblinkingly.

I play the staring game for a minute, but get bored and forfeit to check my phone.

Bummer, Daphne had said while I was in the bath. *I wanted to like him.*

Me too, I think, dropping my phone to the side next to me and settling my hands on Lucy's sides.

She responds by purring, so I think she likes me touching her. *Take that Jakub. At least your pet likes me!*

There's a knock on my bedroom door. I lift my head slightly and see Jakub's face filling the space between the door and the frame.

"What?" I turn my attention back to his cat. Lucy is much more worthy of it. She hasn't tried to screw me over.

"Rafe wants to confirm I can still go with him for his lumberjack thing this week even though he's leaving tonight instead of Thursday like he originally planned," says Jakub, opening the door enough to prop his shoulder against the frame. "Are you okay with that?"

"Why would I care?" Seeing him now, leaning casually in my doorway and looking like he belongs in the lead role of every boy-next-door-style romcom, I have to blink away the sting of tears. I feel like a fool. I was starting to fall for him, not that I would admit that to either him or Daphne, and he turned out not to be at all who I thought he was.

Or rather, he turned out to be exactly who I thought he was. I should have trusted my instincts.

He looks taken aback by my response. "Are you okay being responsible for Lucy while I'm gone?" he says.

"Lucy and I can take care of ourselves just fine."

Lucy gives me a slow blink, as if to tell me that she's worried about me. I can't say I blame her. I'm worried about me too. I can't believe I'd let my guard down and thought Jakub and I might actually be able to be friends. Or more.

But he'd been lying and using me the entire time.

"All right, then," says Jakub slowly. He stands in my doorway for a few moments, maybe waiting for me to stop being so chilly toward him, but I ignore him until he returns the door to its mostly closed state and walks across the hall to his own room.

I lie there in silence for a long time, staring into Lucy's face as she struggles not to nod off on my chest. Jakub doesn't say goodbye, but a while later I hear the front door open and close, followed by silence. Good, this is what I'd wanted. To have him not in my house. To be alone. It's for the best, since I apparently have terrible taste in men.

Chapter Twenty

Lucy cuddles me through the night, and it's surprisingly comforting to have her soft little body curled against me while I sleep. The good night's sleep has me waking up rested and feeling like I can take on the world. Which is exactly how I need to be feeling, since I have to confront my boss about the conversation I overhead.

I stroll right past the clump of desks the other designers and I sit at and straight into Bartholomew's office.

He looks grumpy, but I'm pissed. And pissed trumps grumpy every day of the week.

I drop into the chair in front of his desk and sit with my arms crossed for a good thirty seconds before he finally looks up.

"What?"

"A little bird tells me you're trying to replace me." I try to keep the disdain for him out of my voice, but some ekes out anyway. "Which would be a big mistake. I'm a fantastic graphic designer and I put up with a lot that most people wouldn't. You're lucky to have me."

"You're good, but you're not the best," says my manager, barely looking up at me. "And I'd heard the best was back in town, so I gave him a call. He turned me down this time, so you can stop freaking out that you're being replaced, but give it time. He'll be working here eventually."

Jakub turned him down? That's not how it sounded to me. I'll have to unpack that tidbit later, but right now, I'm pissed off, and it's all focused on my manager for the moment.

"You're a fucking asshole, you know that?" I stand up. "Jakub might be a great painter, and he has an edginess that some brands like, but I'm consistently good. I always deliver on my briefs, and I'm great with clients." The memory of losing my temper at a misogynistic old man from one of my accounts flits through my mind. "Most clients," I amend.

Bartholomew finally trains his attention on me. "Yeah, but if I'm paying top dollar for something, I want it to be the best. And that's not always you," he explains, leaning back in his desk chair with his hands behind his head.

"Top dollar?" Nothing can hold back the laughter that pours out of me. It's bordering on maniacal. "You're lucky to hire any graphic designers at all, with what you offer as a starting salary and no raises."

He smirks. "And yet I've got you."

"Not anymore." I stand up so fast the chair I was sitting in topples over, but I don't care. I don't want to be here another second longer. "I quit."

I stride right over to my desk, or what used to be my desk until a moment ago, and collect the few things I've left here. My coworkers are all staring at me with a mixture of awe and horror. I probably should have closed the door to Bartholomew's office when I went in there. But it's good for my coworkers to hear exactly how he thinks of us. That we're all replaceable in his eyes, and he doesn't truly care about us.

As soon as I'm out the front door, standing on the

sidewalk with my arms full of my things, I'm not sure what to do. I've never been in this position before. The only times I've left jobs, I've had another lined up so I wouldn't go a week without a paycheck.

Now here I am, completely uncertain about my future.

Well, I can't just stand here holding everything forever, so I turn and walk slowly to my car.

Once I'm in the driver's seat, I feel the urge to do something. Go somewhere. My first thought is the café for some decent coffee, but I should figure out my financial future before I spend any unnecessary money.

I'll probably have to get another roommate. Obviously, Jakub can't stay, but it wouldn't be the worst thing to live with someone else. Just for a while, to cut down on my expenses while I find a new job.

Unsure what else to do, I drive back home. As soon as I walk in the front door, Lucy comes down the stairs, her chirpy little hello meows louder than I've heard them before. She probably misses her dad and thought that I was him coming home to her. Poor girl.

"Hey, little girl." She still headbutts my hand a little, but I can see the disappointment in her face. "I get it. Your dad screwed me over too." I give her a few head scratches.

I stomp up the stairs. If I don't have to be at work, there's no reason I shouldn't be in soft pants.

Lucy follows me upstairs. Jakub's door is ajar for her, and she twines around the doorframe, meowing for my attention as I make my way to my own room. I've never looked inside Jakub's room before, because even when he leaves the door open for Lucy, it's not open very wide. But it swings all the way open when she rubs against it now, and I can't resist the urge to peek in. I won't cross the threshold, but if the door is open, there's nothing saying I can't take a quick peek just to see what he's got going on in there.

I'm not sure what I expected to see on the other side of the doorway. But it wasn't this.

Set on an easel in the corner, where I'd never see it without standing directly in the doorway and craning my neck, is a large canvas. It doesn't look complete, but the colors are astounding. They draw me in, and even though I told myself I wouldn't go inside his room, my feet carry me forward until I'm standing before it.

An ancient, burning angel, alight and wielding a sword, about to stab down into the chest of a man kneeling before her. Across her shoulders is a cat who looks suspiciously like Lucy, if Lucy were teal. And on her feet are a pair of roller skates.

My parents named me Seraphine, and I've always hated it. Being angelic never resonated with me. Not when I could be a badass. Yet the way Jakub has portrayed this angel, they look dangerous and in control. This is the Seraphine I've strived to be in my life.

Why the hell is Jakub painting this though? He's not religious as far as I know.

There are several other canvases leaning against the wall, and though I shouldn't, I flip through them. Slowly at first, and then faster, but still careful not to damage them.

They're mostly me. Different versions and in different color aesthetics, but all of them bold and with my same features, streaks of green in the hair no matter the rest of the palette. It's like looking into a very psychedelic mirror.

I cross back to the painting of the angel, and sure enough, there are streaks of green in her hair that I hadn't noticed before.

This is all very overwhelming.

I walk like a zombie into my own room and run a hot bath. I process things better sitting in bubbles. I want to call

Daphne, but she's at work at the bookstore. Just because I've quite my job doesn't mean she can leave hers.

I'm staring at the wall, surrounded by bubbles, when Lucy wanders in and jumps up onto the bathroom counter to stare at me. I stare back. She's just as good to talk to as anyone else, I suppose, though I do feel a little silly using a cat to bounce my thoughts off of.

"Do you know why Jakub kept painting me, Lucy?" I rest my cheek against the edge of the bath as I watch her for a response, but she only blinks at me. "I mean, there were dozens. And they clearly took a long time to paint."

They would have taken months, if not years, to complete. I saw how fast he can complete a painting at the art battle, but these are way more detailed, with more layering. They couldn't have been quick one-offs.

Not ready to go too deep down that path, I switch my thoughts to what my manager had said right before I quit my job. That Jakub had turned down the job offer. But I'd heard him on the phone specifically saying that he would look into working on the Livingston Advantage account.

Unless later he realized it was my account and he'd be stealing my job from me?

I have more questions than answers it seems, and Lucy is not being forthcoming with any secrets she's privy to at the moment.

Grabbing my phone off the ledge, I open up my chat with Rafe. Once I heard that Jakub was considering my job, I'd assumed that either Rafe was also playing me or Jakub had lied to him too. But that seems too far-fetched now that I've seen the paintings. I just have this tiny voice whispering in the back of my mind that maybe Rafe was right about Jakub's feelings for me. But the whole reason I'm in this situation is because I made assumptions without having all the information—from thinking Rafe was the one moving in all the way to now, with Jakub talking to my boss. I need to go straight to the source, but to do that, I need the source's number.

Hey, I don't have Jakub's number. Would you pass it on to me? Or could you give him mine? I text Rafe.

There, I've pulled up my big girl panties once again. I confronted my boss head-on today, and that was scary. Being jobless is scary. But I'm a badass, derby-skating Seraphine just like in Jakub's painting, so I can have a scary conversation with him too.

I rinse off and wrap up in my fluffy bathrobe. It's not like I have a job to go to anymore, so I can wear whatever the hell I want now.

My phone lights up with an unknown number. I don't usually answer, but I did ask Rafe to pass on my number to Jakub, so it could be him. I just didn't think he would respond this quickly. Or that it would be a phone call instead of a text. Who does that?

"Is Lucy okay?" Jakub sounds panicked when I answer. "What's wrong? Are you at the vet now?"

"What? No. Lucy's fine." Does he not think I can handle taking care of one cat by myself? "Why wouldn't she be?"

"Because you told Rafe to have me call you," he says, his voice still strained.

"No, I told him I didn't have your number and asked if he'd send it to me."

"I put it up on the fridge next to the number of Lucy's vet just in case something happened," he says. "Since you didn't call or text me, I assumed maybe you were at the vet with her and hadn't put my number in your phone yet so you couldn't get hold of me."

"I'm not at the vet," I huff. "Lucy is absolutely fine."

"Send me a proof of life picture."

"Fine," I grumble back. I put him on speaker and snap a picture of Lucy, who is sitting in the bathroom doorway. "Happy?" I say once I've sent it to him.

"Yes."

I can't believe I didn't notice that Jakub had put his number and the vet's number on the fridge. I wonder how long ago he did that. If it was yesterday before he left I suppose I can give myself a pass, but if it's been there for weeks...

"So, if you're not calling me about Lucy, what are you calling me about?" Jakub's voice is a lot softer now, more like the tone he'd use when we were lying in the dark in the basement.

"Well, uh"—I suddenly have no idea what to say to him; even though I'm supposed to be being brave and confronting him about the job thing, now that I'm talking to him that feels like it should be an in-person conversation —"it is about Lucy. But it's not an emergency," I rush to clarify when I hear him suck in a breath.

"What kind of thing could be not an emergency, but important enough for you to ask Rafe for my number?" asks Jakub. "Especially when I left it for you on the fridge."

I feel a spike of that same old annoyance I used to feel whenever Jakub was around.

"I didn't see it on the fridge, and you never told me you were leaving it." I tamp down the irritation. It's not going to accomplish anything. "It's just...Lucy misses you."

It's a weak excuse for calling, but it's all I can think of, and it's probably true. Especially given the way she's taken to following me around since he's been gone.

"Oh, does she?" Jakub chuckles in my ear, making my stomach flip.

"I mean, she's used to you being around, I guess." I was getting used to him being around, too.

"Did she sleep with you last night?"

"Of course. I wasn't going to make her sleep alone. I'm not some heartless monster." My mind flashes to the painting on the easel in Jakub's room. "But, um, she still keeps looking out the window for you. And going in your bedroom and meowing."

"Did you look in there?" he says sharply. When I don't reply, he adds, "I mean, to see if there was something upsetting her?"

"No," I respond, maybe a little too quickly. "I assumed she's wondering why you aren't in there."

"And then after Lucy went into my room, she made it clear that she missed me enough that you had to call me," says Jakub. "For her."

"Yes." A beat. "So, um, when are you coming home? So I can let Lucy know. We didn't really have a chance to go over details, since Rafe decided to leave early and you had to rush." Is it fair of me to pin the blame for our not talking on Rafe? Probably not. But I don't want to admit over the phone that I was being bitchy because of unfounded assumptions.

"The competition doesn't end until Sunday afternoon, so I probably won't be able to get back until well after dark by the time we pack everything up and get on the road." Jakub is back to using his basement voice, now that he's not worrying I snooped in his room. A stab of guilt hits me because that's exactly what I did, but I shove it aside. Too late to undo it. I'll have to figure out how to tell him later.

"Okay, that's good to know. I'll make sure to pass that on to Lucy so she isn't worried about you." And that gives me some time to figure out what I'm going to say when I see Jakub again.

"Good." He pauses, the silence on the line thick between us. "Was there anything else?"

"No." I'm not sure what else to say. It's not like I can tell him I miss him. Or that I'm sorry for listening in on his phone call and assuming he was trying to steal my job, even if it was a natural conclusion based on our past interactions.

"Okay, well. I'll see you then, then."

"Yeah. Lucy says bye." I hold the phone out to Lucy and she actually meows into the receiver.

Jakub is laughing softly on the other side of the call as I hang up.

I look down at the damp robe I'm still wrapped in. "Okay, little girl, time for comfy clothes," I say to Lucy as I throw on sweatpants and a hoodie. "We have six days until your dad gets home, and I don't have a job. What do you say to a *Brits Who Bake* marathon?"

Silently, Lucy stands and glides out of the room. "I'll take that as a yes."

Chapter Twenty-One

"So how did it feel to bum around the house all week?" teases Daphne, sipping her coffee.

"I wasn't bumming around." I roll my eyes, but I still laugh. "I only watched five seasons of *Brits Who Bake*, but it's because Lucy loved it."

"Does that mean you're going to start baking?" Daphne's eyes light up at the potential for homemade pastries.

"Probably not. Instead of spending time in the kitchen, I've been on my computer applying for new jobs." Not that it's done me any good. Few places are hiring, and of the ad agencies that are, I've either already worked there and left or other graphic designer friends have told me horror stories about them.

"Well, if you get bored at home, come by the bookstore. We're looking at hosting a few more community events and we need better graphics than we have now," says Daphne, running her hand over the reddish-blond braid that rests on her shoulder.

"Thank you." I set down my mug and really look at Daphne. She's such a great friend. This is the second time that she is offering me a lifeline so I don't drown, and she does it so casually. "I really appreciate it."

Daphne shrugs as if it's no big deal, but it is.

"The bookstore can be your safe space, especially once Jakub comes back. Do you know when that is so you can brace yourself?"

"Tonight," I say, watching the counter. The new barista is working, and she's getting better. There isn't a huge line today.

"Are you excited?" Daphne draws out the last word, grinning obnoxiously.

I shake my head. "I don't know. He didn't steal my job, but it certainly sounded like he was considering it, so it's still something big between us. And if we can't trust each other, can we really work together as something more than friends?" This has been on my mind all week. It hasn't helped that Jakub hasn't texted me at all since our phone call. He'd heart-reacted to the picture of Lucy after we hung up, but that's it. "Plus, I don't know what to do about the paintings. Do I tell him I saw them? Or pretend they don't exist?"

"Those paintings could slide from adorable to suspicious real fast," says Daphne. "I vote you ask him about those first thing when he gets back."

"Yeah, you're probably right," I say. "Ugh. That's not going to be fun. It would be easier if I knew how I feel about him."

"You do know. You just don't want to admit it to yourself."

I glare at her. "Even if that were true, what am I supposed to do about it?"

"Do you need to do anything?"

"You're saying I should do nothing?" That doesn't sound like Daphne. Although with the way she's been doing nothing about her crush on Rowan, it could be her own M.O. talking.

She shrugs. "You don't have to make it be some big huge thing. You could keep living together, but be open about liking each other. It'd be the same thing you've been doing, but better because then everything is out in the open instead of secret."

"It would be nice not to have secrets," I agree. "And maybe we could work on trusting each other." I sit up straighter and point at her. "But enough about my love life complications. Let's talk about yours."

"What about mine?" Daphne's mug clatters in the saucer when she sets it down and some coffee sloshes over the lip.

"When are you going to stop sitting in the corner mooning over Rowan and actually have a conversation with him?" Last night's party was no different from every other Saturday night. Daphne made googly eyes at Rowan from across the room, he didn't notice at all, and then he disappeared upstairs with someone else. "He's never going to realize how great you are if he doesn't have a chance to get to know you."

"He knows me," she protests.

"He doesn't, but even if he did, that's not really making your case," I tell her. I reach out and grab her hand, which is covered in retro mood rings. "I want you to be happy. You deserve that. And if Rowan is what will make you happy, then I'm going to do what I can to help you get him. But you've got to help me help you."

"I don't need help. I'm fine with how things are." Daphne doesn't get stubborn very often, but when she does, she's downright mulish, and I can tell that's the path we're headed down if I keep pushing. I've already voiced my opinion so I'm not going to say anything more. Besides, I've already made a mess of my own situation, so who am I to judge her for hers?

My entire body is buzzing with the knowledge that Jakub is coming home tonight. I can't settle. I keep wandering around the house, noticing the little things he's changed or added—mostly cat things, like Lucy's tower, a few beds, her toys that are strewn around the floor. All of it is evidence that although this is technically my house, it's now a home that doesn't entirely belong to me. It's a combination of all of us now.

My phone vibrates on the coffee table and I dive to check it in case it's Jakub.

It's not, though. It's Daphne. *Bad weather tonight.*

For once, the news of a storm has me excited instead of cowering. Jakub is coming home. We'll go to the basement, and he'll comfort me and make me feel safe.

I send her a quick thank you and consider texting Jakub to let him know, but I don't want to come across as desperate. I go upstairs to grab my pillow and hesitate outside of Jakub's room. Should I get his too? Will he be upset if he knows I went into his room and saw the angel painting? I decide it's worth it. He might not come looking for me, but maybe he'll come looking for his pillow.

Once the pull-out sofa is set up in the basement, I go back up and call for Lucy because she didn't follow me downstairs. I also turn on the lamp in the foyer so Jakub doesn't come home to a dark house.

I spot Lucy camped out in her hammock by the window, clearly waiting for her dad to come home to her.

"Come on, little girl. It's going to get dangerous outside, so you've got to come downstairs where it's safe." I scoop her up, thankful she doesn't freak out in my arms as I carry her to the basement and close the door. "We're going to sleep down here tonight."

I climb into bed, and she comes over to check out her dad's pillow. This sofa bed really is the worst. Between the lumpy springs and the storm and waiting for Jakub, I'm not sure how I'm going to sleep tonight.

After a while, I hear the front door open and close, and there are footsteps upstairs. My entire body thrums with excitement, but I don't move. If anything, I pretend even harder to be asleep. Lucy, on the other hand, does a big stretch and then jumps off the bed to prance up the stairs.

This is the moment of decision. Is Jakub going to go sleep upstairs with the smaller pillow I left up there for him, or is he going to come down here looking for the one he's brought down the other times? Did he check the weather radar? Does he even know there's a storm? I should have texted him.

I hear him going up the stairs to the second floor, and when he doesn't immediately come down, my entire body sags into the mattress. I put myself out there and he didn't take the bait. Maybe Rafe was wrong about him having feelings for me, or maybe I fucked it up when I was bratty the night he left.

Lucy doesn't seem to have gotten the message though, because when the basement door didn't immediately open for her, she started meowing and sticking her paw underneath to rattle the door in its frame.

Footsteps sound again above my head. Then the basement door opens.

"Hey, my love, are you staying safe from the storm?" Jakub coos softly at the top of the stairs.

Lucy's answering purr is so loud, I can hear it all the way down here.

Jakub begins to descend the stairs, and I close my eyes, pretending to be asleep. It's one thing to bring his pillow downstairs, it's another to let him know that I've stayed up waiting for him.

The bed dips, and I have to practically cling to my side of the bed to keep from rolling toward him.

"I know you're not asleep, so there's no use in pretending," says Jakub, snuggling up behind me.

"No, I'm sleeping," I say, keeping my eyes closed.

"Oh, well, in that case, I definitely believe you."

"Of course you should believe me. *I'm* very trustworthy," I insist, abandoning the pretense of sleep to look over my shoulder. The light from the kitchen bleeds down the stairs, backlighting him so all I can see is his profile.

"And I'm not?" he asks, brushing a strand of hair from my face.

"I heard you talking to my boss about taking my job. And there are a lot of paintings in your room that make me think you might be a stalker," I point out.

"First of all, your boss called me. And I did take the call, but mostly out of curiosity. Don't judge me for this, but I'm scoping out the market." Jakub drops his forehead onto my shoulder. "I really like being freelance, but I've been thinking more and more about opening up my own ad agency where we prioritize the art and branding and don't have to deal with the bullshit that happens at most ad agencies."

"Oh." I can't fault him for that. One of the first things we were taught in our classes was to do our market research. "Any chance you might have room for another graphic designer at this new agency? Because I have kind of found myself unemployed as of this week."

He lifts his head to look down at me. "Have you, now? What happened?"

"It's possible that I confronted my boss about the phone call he had with you, and then rage-quit when he had the balls to suggest that I'm not the best graphic designer he knows and also that he doesn't underpay his employees."

He laughs. "Well, if and when I get this new agency off the ground, you'll be the first person I call."

"And what about the stalker paintings?" I ask. "Why so many?"

"I like your face." I can feel Jakub's grin against my shoulder. "Besides, I think they helped me find the truth."

"What truth?"

"That you like me," he says confidently.

"Who said that?" I'm sure Daphne wouldn't rat me out like that, even if she did tell him to shoot his shot with me. Maybe Rafe, if he overheard us talking at the café at some point?

"Are you implying you've chosen to sleep on this awful mattress on nights that no storm is forecasted, just in case?"

"There are very few nights the possibility of a storm is exactly zero." Which is true. "And maybe I like this bed."

"There's no way that's true, this pull-out sofa is the worst. I think you like the fact that I join you."

"There is actually going to be bad weather tonight. Daphne texted me." It's too scary to just come out and admit that he's right, that I don't hate him—that I like him, quite a lot.

Jakub rolls onto his back to stare up at the ceiling. "Are you saying that all the nights we've slept down here, it was only because of the weather? Because if so, I'm going to go back upstairs and leave you down here. I can't take another night on this mattress if it's just as a precaution against some weather."

"But it's really going to storm!" I sit up and stare down at him in the dim light from the kitchen. Surely, he wouldn't leave me down here alone in bad weather. He's supposed to comfort me.

"I'm not afraid." Jakub shrugs and starts to climb off the mattress on the other side.

Diving across the bed, I grab hold of his shirt to keep him here. "But I am," I admit.

"Of storms?"

"Yes."

"That's all?"

I'm still clutching his shirt, and he's not moving away but he's not coming back, either.

"And..."

"And?" he prompts, and I can hear the grin in his voice.

"And liking you," I whisper, my entire body tense as I wait for his reaction.

"See? Was that so hard?" Jakub rolls so he's back on the bed and we're laying face to face.

"You're a smug asshole, you know that?"

He laughs, and the tension drains out of me. I had thought this would all be so much easier if I didn't have to look him in the eyes. But it turns out that admitting it's what I want is sort of freeing, and much nicer than pretending I don't want it.

"I liked our rivalry," I admit. "I'm really good at it."

"I know." Jakub brushes his hand along my face, sweeping away more hair that's escaped my topknot. "But we're really good at other things together too."

Jakub brushes his thumb across my lower lip to stop me from arguing with him, and that little touch sends a shiver through me. In all the times we've had sex down here, we've never kissed, and suddenly I find myself desperate to press my lips to his. I tilt my chin toward him, wondering if he'll read my mind or if he'll make me say it out loud.

Slowly, Jakub leans in and follows his thumb with a brush of his lips. It's soft and sweet, and almost a test. It probably is a test, to see if I run. But when he goes to pull back, I chase after him. He can't give me something so wonderful only to take it away with the next breath.

"I do have one request though," says Jakub, holding my chin to keep me near, but not letting me kiss him.

"What's that?" My breath is coming heavier, and I can't take my eyes off his lips.

"Can we please, please sleep upstairs tonight? The weather isn't supposed to be that bad, and I'll keep you safe," he says. "And then tomorrow we can go buy a new pull-out sofa for down here, because this one is shit on my back."

"You promise to keep me safe?"

"I wouldn't suggest it if I thought otherwise."

"Okay." I take a deep breath. I can try it once. For him. "These springs really are hard and pokey."

Jakub leans in for a searing kiss. "As soon as we get upstairs, I can show you something else hard and pokey," he says against my lips, and a laugh escapes me in spite of my apprehension about the storm.

"Your room or mine?" asks Jakub, rolling off the mattress and grabbing our pillows.

"Can we sleep in mine?" I ask, following him up the stairs, appreciative of the way his jeans hug his ass. "It'd be weird to sleep in yours surrounded by so many paintings of myself."

"We can do that," he says. "I personally enjoy having so many of you watch me, but none of them compare to the real you, flesh and blood."

When we reach my room, Jakub tosses our pillows on my bed and pulls me in for a kiss. No longer testing, but hot and demanding. It's like now that we've finally given in, we're having a hard time pulling apart.

Lucy comes trilling into the bedroom, and Jakub pulls away from me.

"Not now, my little girl." He scoops up Lucy in his arms, plants a kiss on her forehead and sets her down just outside my door. "Mom and Dad need a little alone time."

"She could come in," I argue. "I don't want her to be scared when the thunder starts."

"Later," Jakub assures me. "She's just a little girl and we're about to do some very dirty things. Besides, I want you all to myself."

"Oh, really?" I turn off the overhead light so we're plunged into darkness, then reach out and find the hem of his shirt. I want all of the dirty promises right now.

Jakub lets me lift his argyle sweater over his head, lifting mine over my head at the same time. We tangle together, laughing, and he backs me toward my bed. The backs of my knees hit it, and we fall onto the quilt.

Jakub reaches over to turn on my bedside lamp, its soft light falling over us.

Reflexively, I hold my arms to cover myself. "Why did you do that?"

"I'm done with the dark," he says, reaching out for my hands and setting them on him instead. "I want to be able to see you this time."

Smiling down at me, Jakub looks me in the eye as he tugs my sleep pants down my legs and unbuttons his jeans, letting them pool around his ankles. He leans forward and I rise up to meet him as he brushes another kiss over my lips, but one kiss isn't enough for either of us. We both want it all.

Bonus Scene

Thank you so much for reading *The Wrong Roommate*. Didn't get enough of Sera and Jakub? Check out this sweet and spicy little scene from when they come home from the roller derby championships.

Ready for more romance in the world of the Tea City Rollers? Keep an eye out for *The Wrong Piece*:

Daphne enjoys the quiet things in life: reading books, listening to emo music, and winning jigsaw puzzle competitions. Rowan can barely manage the local roller derby team, let alone his life, and when his grandmother's birthday party rolls around, he knows his family is going to give him grief about his bachelor lifestyle the way they always do. A fake girlfriend could solve that problem, but things are about to get complicated because Rowan has no idea that Daphne's goal is to turn this fake relationship into the real thing. And she's known for solving complicated puzzles fast.

About the Author

Alby Blake is a grant award winning, midwest romance author who spends her days researching ways to embarrass her characters and trying to drink as much tea as possible. If she's not writing, she may be in the garden or admiring her cats.

Also by Alby Blake

Bro Amazing

Bro Smooth

Bro Awesome